Darcy's Tale

Volume I

Into Hertfordshire

By

Stanley Michael Hurd

© 2014 by Stanley M. Hurd.

All rights reserved, including reproduction in whole or in part, in print or electronic media, except by Amazon and its affiliates for the purposes of marketing the work through their online program.

This is a work of fiction, and all characters, character names, places, and events were created as such to meet the needs of the author's imagination. Any resemblance to any person or persons, living or dead, or any locale, or any event, is purely coincidental.

Publisher: Stanley M. Hurd

Second edition, published 2014.

ISBN 13 978-0-9910382-4-4

Cover design: J. E. Hurd

Many friends have made this possible; a special thanks to my daughters, who were my Editors in Chief, and my wife, who was my long-suffering reader, companion, sounding board, and, in sum, long-suffering mate, period.

I also owe a great deal to my friends at the Derbyshire Writers' Guild for their scholarship, aid, and encouragement. May you live long, may your numbers grow, and may you be called home to Pemberley in the end.

*A man is rich who has a good wife —
I have wealth beyond counting.
Thank you, KB.*

FOREWORD

This second edition has been substantially re-edited for anachronisms and Americanisms; our thanks to those sharp-eyed readers who have helped make this edition possible.

Darcy's Tale is presented in three volumes, as was the original *Pride and Prejudice* 200 years earlier; this has been done both for reasons of historical accuracy and because the story naturally divides itself into three major sections.

The correspondence between Darcy and his sister is included in its entirety in the Correspondence section, as certain letters had no place in the events of the book. They have been included to allow the reader to follow each letter as it was written, without the shifts in time and circumstance which occurred during the intervals between writings. In an age when communications took weeks to complete, letters held their own internal chronology, quite independent of external events; the reader is invited to enjoy this more stately rhythm of life by following the correspondents' individual stories as described in their letters, in the order in which they were exchanged.

Prologue

*****

Mr. Charles Bingley to Mr. Fitzwilliam Darcy
Manchester Square
September 6, —

Dear Darcy,

Greetings from the South, my friend! I trust all is well in Derbyshire and you are enjoying your usual good health; please give your dear sister my best regards.

Well, now! I must ask for your congratulations, as I am about to join you amongst the ranks of England's landed families. I have taken Netherfield Hall, the property in Hertfordshire that Delacroix mentioned to us in Town last July! I went down to see it for myself last Friday, and it is eminently suited to my needs. Fine hangars of timber, just enough variety in the lay of the land to lend interest to the hunt, and enough arable to be profitable — given an infusion of resources. I had my agent execute the lease on Monday. I have sent my man Roberts down to hire the servants, and the Hall should be habitable by the end of the month.

I should very much like to have your opinion of the property. When do you plan to be back in Town? We could ride down to see it together, or even make a stay of it and get some shooting in if you like.

Your Obedient &c.
Charles Bingley

Into Hertfordshire

*****

Mr. Fitzwilliam Darcy to Mr. Charles Bingley
> Pemberley House,
> September 9, —

Dear Bingley,

Never one to do things by halves, are you? My dear Sir—you saw it for one day? Good timber and pleasant scenery do not make a manor! "Enough arable" is well and good, but what about drainage? Not to mention the drains in the Hall. Do you have any idea what a disaster it is to have a houseful of guests when the drains refuse to do their office? And the cistern, in what condition is the cistern? Your new servants will desert you *en masse* if they must carry every quart of bathwater up stairs by hand. Your blithe mention of an "infusion of resources" I find a bit troubling, but that, after all, is your look-out. If you want to spend your capital on a leased property, well, I am sure that any resultant impecunities will have a most salutary effect on your character.

I shall be back in Town after Michaelmas quarter-day; I am obliged to remain at Pemberley until then to settle the harvest affairs. The harvest this year has been exceedingly generous and I shall have certain affairs to set in motion once I get to London, but they should not take long. I shall look forward to placing myself at your disposal any time after the second week of October.

Truly, my dear Bingley, I hope from my heart that the property will prove itself worthy of your most sanguine hopes, and that my more jaundiced eyes will see it even as do your own. I look forward to seeing it, and you, very soon.

Yours faithfully, &c.

Fitzwilliam Darcy

Prologue

*****

Miss Georgiana Darcy to Mr. Fitzwilliam Darcy
[1]Pemberley
October 7, —

Dearest Brother,

Thank you for sending Mrs. Annesley to me; she is very gentle and obliging. We spend time every day on my music and reading. Pemberley has been cold since you left, but as I have no wish to go out this is no hardship on me. Colonel Fitzwilliam has stopped in to visit, although you are doubtless already aware of that. He is all kindness, but his solicitude is a constant reminder of my transgressions, and, indeed, I need no such reminder. The Colonel means well, I know, and next to you he is the dearest of my relations, but I do not deserve his concern and my spirits are not sufficient to make me good company. I do not ask a boon, Brother, as I merit none, but I do think my cousin's time would be better spent elsewhere. Perhaps, dear Brother, if you see this as I do, you might suggest to him a different and more worthwhile endeavour? I cannot bear to have him waste his time and care on one such as I.
Your devoted sister,
Georgiana

*****

Mr. Fitzwilliam Darcy to Miss Georgiana Darcy
Grosvenor Square
October 10, —

Dearest Sister,

---

[1] The interested reader will find all the letters between Darcy and his sister in the Correspondence section at the end of the book.

Into Hertfordshire

My dear, gentle Georgiana, your letter grieves me more than words can express. Your pain is my doing, entirely; I neglected you and trusted others to perform duties that properly belonged to me. Mrs. Younge abused my trust while you were at Ramsgate, it is true; but she could not have done so had not I, with an imprudence altogether inexcusable in one of my years, accepted her recommendations without sufficient enquiry. Nor had I prepared you as I ought to have done for such men as he. I knew him for what he was, yet never sought to inform you, not only of *his* character, but even of the existence of such predatory men. My excuse is that I had thought to preserve your innocence and spare you this knowledge, but I see now that that is like sparing the knowledge of fire: we encounter it everywhere, and if we are not taught caution it will do us grave injury. My Mother, I know, would not have left you defenceless in this way, and I berate myself for not having foreseen this need. I, who pride myself on my understanding, have failed utterly in its application.

I have allowed you to be badly burned, and I pray to God that the pain will subside and the scars will fade, for yours is the sweetest nature Heaven ever sent to Earth; if I have allowed such an angelic disposition to suffer permanent damage I shall never forgive myself. Dearest, you must believe me: you did no more than accept the lies of a man who could deceive even one so worthy as Father, as you must now realise he was wholly deceived by the man. And you must remember, as I certainly do, that it was your own goodness that made you acknowledge to me your planned elopement, for the pain you knew it

Prologue

would give me. You are too good: you cannot allow even your most pressing desires to harm another. Please, please consider my words, Dearest, and believe that I am,
Your most loving and contrite brother,
Fitzwilliam Darcy

Chapter One

On a Thursday morning in mid-October, Mr. Fitzwilliam Darcy sat in his library overlooking Grosvenor Square in London, studying in a desultory fashion some of the details of his affairs. The business of the year had gone well and the coffers were pleasingly full, and he was enjoying a not unreasonable amount of that satisfaction which comes from seeing one's efforts justly rewarded. But the financial outlook was, in fact, very nearly the only part of the past year upon which he could reflect with any complacence. It had all begun with the Season the previous winter: more so than any other in his memory, it had been one long, dreary round of sterile society and empty pomp. Darcy was one of the most eligible bachelors in London, and was therefore much sought after by the misses and matrons of Society. The matrons urged their daughters on his acquaintance, and the misses fluttered around him at every dinner and ball. London's Season was little less than a matrimonial fair for people of his age and condition, and, while not an excessively social man, he would in general accept two or three invitations a week; perhaps rather less than that in this last year. He was not by nature attracted to the *ton* — although his wealth and connections placed him in the first circles — and he had no urgent need of a wife, so he felt free to pick and choose from among the invitations he received; still, he remembered to advantage the happiness of his own parents' marriage, and had always entertained the hope that he would, at some time in the indefinite future, enjoy the same benefits. Lately though, that hope had been dwindling. The unfortunate reality he observed in the married couples of his acquaintance, and the promise of the matrimonial state offered by the women he knew, was far from the ideal he had observed in his parents' union. He

Into Hertfordshire

was sensible enough to be conscious of the want of true character in those Society misses so abundant in London, and philosopher enough to find some small entertainment in the unwitting ironies and absurdities of the women who surrounded him. What he did not realise was how very isolated his life was becoming, and that the reason he was secure against the women of his circle was the fact that his own more serious nature was very much out of place amongst the intrigues and inconsequentialities of Society. All this summed itself up in him as an indistinct, but growing, dissatisfaction with things in general, and with social intercourse in particular.

Then there had been the disastrous events of July. Having gone to Ramsgate to make a surprise visit to his young sister, Georgiana, he had arrived to find her on the very eve of an elopement! And the man! —George Wickham, the son of his father's steward; Wickham, whom Darcy had known since childhood, and moreover, known to be a thoroughly deceitful and dishonourable individual. Darcy had early on discovered that Wickham was, by some cruel chance, his own personal Nemesis; always possessed of a great deal of charm, which he would wield to his advantage at every opportunity, Wickham had an extraordinary capacity for lying which was exceeded only by his credibility while doing so. Darcy was not so blest with social grace and ease, being rather too forthright in his manner to be generally pleasing, so it often came about that, though Darcy was devoted to the strictest truth, Wickham's lies carried a sweeter taste and, therefore, a greater conviction. Many and many a time had Darcy gone to his father to report some base act of Wickham's, only to earn the frustration and shame of his father's disbelief; Wickham had so thoroughly seduced his father's reason in his favour that he was always able to wriggle, eel-like, out of any difficulty. The smirk Wickham always gave him over his father's shoulder at these moments angered Darcy with the unal-

Chapter I

loyed intensity of youth, but he could never manage to convince his father of his protégé's unworthiness. He had eventually taken refuge by distancing himself from Wickham as much and as often as possible, but even this brought with it a degree of mortification, in the form of his father's censure for his coldness to one whom the elder Mr. Darcy thought so deserving.

Wickham was one who would always take more than he was offered, and had quickly managed to exhaust his father's small legacy, a rather larger one left him by Darcy's father, and a settlement from Darcy himself made in honour of his father's wishes, which combined would have kept a prudent man for ten years. Having already petitioned Darcy unsuccessfully for additional funds, Wickham had obviously decided to worm his way into the Darcy fortune through marriage, and Georgiana was ready to hand. Her ruination and the degradation of the Darcy name meant nothing to him, so long as he could supply himself with the money he desired.

At Ramsgate, when Darcy had discovered them, he had for the first time in his life seriously considered issuing a challenge; this treacherous attempt to injure his sister and, indeed, his entire family, had swept him up in a murderous wrath that had astonished him by its fury. All that kept him from it was the eventual realization that to *afficher* the affair publically with a duel was to spread the scandal throughout his acquaintance and beyond. There had remained nothing to do but to escort Georgiana back to their estate in Derbyshire and try his best to repair the damage done to her heart. Thankfully, nothing of the matter had reached outside ears; his cousin, Colonel Edmund Fitzwilliam, who was joined with him in Georgiana's care, was the only other soul who knew of the intended elopement. At least, Darcy hoped that this was so.

Georgiana herself had been completely overcome with heartache and remorse. She could barely tolerate being in

Into Hertfordshire

Darcy's presence, as her sense of guilt over the ruin she had almost brought down on them all was made all the more acute by his gentle treatment of her: convinced as she was of her unworthiness, his kindness served only to hold up the mirror of her disgrace. Darcy had eventually left Pemberley for Town several weeks early, just to spare her pain.

Concern for his sister and the indefinite sense of emptiness in his own life oppressed Darcy's spirits during unoccupied moments, and consequently he worked hard to have as few such moments as possible. His diligence to his affairs in recent months therefore had had a twofold purpose: to improve the family's fortunes, yes; but also to push away from himself a black mood that always hovered in the back reaches of his mind, waiting to descend upon him whenever his thoughts were free to turn to his own condition.

With cares such as these to afflict him, it can be no wonder that he had sought relief in solitude and activity. But now the harvest affairs were over and he was settled in London; having no business to absorb his time, and solitude in London being a near impossibility, he rather imagined that the diversions of the place and season would serve him well. His social duties were sure to rise, and, he rather hoped, would provide the distraction he had enjoyed through his attention to his affairs.

He had just done with his last business of the morning when the sound of the knocker echoed through the house. Since very few knew he was in Town and it was rather early in the day, he assumed it was some concern of the household. However, the sound of footsteps approaching down the hall heralded an arrival at the library door.

"Mr. Bingley," announced the butler, Goodwin. His countenance remained perfectly impassive, as always, but an air of approbation for this particular visitor seemed to waft from him. Mr. Charles Bingley was Darcy's closest friend, and very nearly his only close friend in London.

Chapter I

Darcy's acquaintance was large, but his intimates were few, and in Bingley he found the only person outside his own family in whom he could confide, and on whom he might rely.

Bingley's family money had come through trade, but Bingley was thoroughly the gentleman, and of a most complaisant temperament. Most of those who knew them both wondered that so strong a bond could subsist between two such opposite characters: Bingley was all that was amiable, while Darcy was renowned for his reserve. They lived not far apart in London and had met, as people do, in the course of an evening's entertainment; they were introduced by their hostess and seated together at supper, and the rest followed naturally. Bingley was undeterred by—indeed, he seemed altogether unaware of—Darcy's reserved manner: he spoke to him as though they had been the best of friends since childhood. The novelty of being thus addressed, combined with Bingley's good sense, informed mind, and affability, produced in Darcy a most favourable impression; this was reinforced by the discovery that Bingley belonged to the same college as himself, and shared an admiration for Darcy's favourite professor. With all this in their favour, it was the work of but a very few weeks before they were every where seen together. Darcy, being the older of the two, and admittedly the cleverer, looked out for Bingley's interests with care, and Bingley's natural diffidence and obliging nature allowed him to be led by Darcy in many ways. Bingley, on the other hand, had the wiser heart, and made return to Darcy through his warm affection, great good humour, and by continually forcing Darcy out of his own constricted existence and into society. During this last year Darcy had relied on his good nature extensively to help ward off his tendency to lowness.

"Bingley!" Darcy welcomed his friend, rising from his cluttered desk. "Hail to England's latest country squire!"

Into Hertfordshire

Bingley, whose open and pleasant face bore a famously large smile, came through the door and shook hands happily with his friend. "Darcy!" cried he, "how good it is to see you. It has been an age! I have not seen you since you left us for Ramsgate last summer. Oh, and I say! you never told us how your surprise visit to Miss Darcy went off."

A cloud passed briefly across Darcy's face and he shot a cautious glance at Bingley; seeing nothing but a friendly, confiding countenance, his own brow cleared. "Ramsgate, it was…indeed…" he said in his momentary confusion. "My sister was thoroughly surprised by my arrival, I assure you. I found her, though…not in spirits…and so took her back to Pemberley directly after." He returned quickly to his first topic: "But here you are, and set to become a landowner! Squire Bingley, commissioner of the peace and patron of the parish! Or have you done another about-turn and decided to leave off?"

"No, no," replied Bingley with a self-satisfied air, taking a seat and stretching out his legs, "I have no thought but to proceed."

Darcy arched a brow. "What, a full month gone and you still steady to your purpose? The heavens must be reeling!"

"Come, Darcy, I am not as bad as all that. In any event, the countryside is delightful, and I have met several of my new neighbours already; they seem a decent lot."

"And how many beautiful country misses have you fallen in love with?"

"Nary a one, so far," replied Bingley, his smile making another appearance. "But I have heard rumours of several very pretty girls in the neighbourhood. I mean to track them to their lair this coming week. I am to attend a ball…well, an assembly, really…Tuesday next." He looked at Darcy optimistically. "I *am* hoping to persuade you to accompany me."

Chapter I

"Bingley," Darcy groaned, "you know how I hate balls...and at a village assembly! Great Heavens!"

"It is not such a *very* small village," Bingley protested, encouraged by not receiving a frank negative. "Meryton is quite a decent-sized little market-town. Caroline says she will go, but only if you do." He looked hopefully at his friend.

At this Darcy's shoulders sagged imperceptibly; he saw defeat looming before him. Bingley's shot, loosed at random, had found the chink in his armour. His friends could always urge Darcy to action on the strength of his sense of duty and propriety, especially where a lady was concerned. Not that this was Bingley's intent, nor did he even realise it; his own desire for society, particularly in company with ladies, was so constant, so honest and forthright, that he often carried his friend along while being completely unaware that Darcy was acting contrary to his own wishes—the nicety of Darcy's scruples quite escaped Bingley's notice. Miss Caroline Bingley, Mr. Bingley's younger sister, was not a great favourite with Darcy, but he had admitted her into his acquaintance willingly for Bingley's sake, and over time had even allowed her a degree of familiarity unusual in his general acquaintance. Having thus admitted her, he recognised his duty to play the gentleman to her—at measured intervals, at any rate. But though his attendance at this country affair might be unavoidable, Darcy had no wish to let Caroline Bingley think she could call his tune. "I shall consider it," he replied evenly. "But in any event I stand ready to accompany you into the wilds of Hertfordshire. I am most anxious to see what you are getting yourself into."

"Oh, that is excellent, Darcy! Would it suit you to go down on Monday?"

"Admirably."

"That is all I could hope for! But now I must run; I am sorry I cannot stay longer, but will you come round for din-

Into Hertfordshire

ner on Sunday? Caroline would be delighted, and it would certainly brighten *my* afternoon."

"I thank you for the invitation, but will you allow me to exchange it for one of my own? I have been haring all over London since the moment I arrived, and I was looking forward to a bit of quiet this weekend. Come and dine with me, instead."

"With very great pleasure!" Bingley agreed with alacrity. He looked questioningly at Darcy. "Do you feel the need to extend your invitation to my sisters?"

"'Sisters'? Are both your sisters in Town, then?"

"Yes, Hurst has been staying here for his mother's sake. She has been feeling poorly, or so she says, and Hurst and Louisa have been up to see to things for her. They said she was on the mend, though. Caroline invited them for Sunday, without discussing it with me, mind you, so I should be happy to forego the pleasure in favour of dinner with you."

"Done, then. Shall we say six o'clock?"

Bingley agreed and the matter was settled. Offering his compliments, repeating his happiness at seeing his friend, as well as his gratitude for Darcy's obligingness, he slowly worked his way to the door. When the door finally closed on his effusiveness, Darcy instructed Goodwin to pass the word of his travel arrangements for the Monday following.

Chapter Two

*E*arly Sunday evening Darcy and Bingley were doing the right thing by an especially fine roast of venison while Bingley responded to Darcy's catechism on his new property.

"Now then," Darcy began, "tell me about this acquisition of yours. What size is it?"

"It is rather small, really, only about a thousand acres. But a good half of it is sound farmland. And, to anticipate your next question, no, I do not know about the drainage. It is not flat land, though, and I saw no standing water in the fields. Does that say anything?"

"It says you can tell the difference between Hertfordshire and Lincolnshire; I am not sure it says much else," was Darcy's wry reply. "A field can go sour in a valley just as well as in a fen. What crops were there this year?"

"I am no farmer," Bingley protested. "I cannot tell one type of stubble from another once the harvest is in!"

"Nor should I expect you to," allowed Darcy. "But surely it was all laid out in the ledgers."

Bingley found a sudden deep interest in the food on his plate. When the moment stretched until it was obvious there would be no reply, Darcy lifted his eyes heavenward. "You did not even trouble yourself to look at the ledgers? Bingley!"

"But the property *looks* so very prosperous! The manor house is lovely, and the park and shrubbery are well-maintained," Bingley defended himself. "Surely that proves the estate can support itself."

"Proves it? No, it suggests it; more than likely it was built by just such another Londoner as yourself, with more ready than prudence, who sank the lot into a pretty manor for a shooting box only to lose the whole thing because it haemorrhaged money at every turn." He turned a sharp eye

Into Hertfordshire

on Bingley. "In your letter last month you said it would need an infusion of capital; how did you arrive at that conclusion, ignorant as you are of the finances of the place?"

"How the Devil you remember these things is entirely beyond me," muttered Bingley. "I know it pleases you to fancy yourself one of London's leading intellects, but let me tell you it is very rude behaviour in common usage." When Darcy did not release him from his expectant gaze, Bingley grudgingly admitted: "The leasing agent told me it would."

"The leasing agent!" Darcy exclaimed. "Great Heavens, man...you let the other fellow's agent tell you about the finances of the place? I thought your family was in trade! Did your father teach you nothing?"

"You need not take it like that", Bingley bridled. "My father did not wish me to engage in trade, he intended for me to be a gentleman-said he had made enough for both of us."

"I dare say he had," agreed Darcy. "But what about *your* sons, and their sons? Let me tell you something my father told *me*. He said that a family's fortunes were either rising or falling—they never stay the same. If you are not increasing your capital, you are losing it. You can see it in every corner of the Kingdom, where some ancient landed family can barely keep up its liabilities to the Crown. There is nothing particularly gentlemanly about living beyond your means, whatever the current fashion for excesses might be. Never squander capital! Getting that thought into my head was my father's last legacy to me, and by Heaven, if need be I shall nag you into an understanding of it just as he did me." He fixed Bingley with a fierce eye.

Bingley fought back gamely: "Come now, Darcy, you cannot claim that Pemberley is what any one might call a Spartan, utilitarian sort of place."

"No," Darcy replied. "But neither is it a pleasure-palace. You know yourself that the family quarters constitute considerably less than half the manor. The rest is given over to the requisite chambers for guests, social events, and administrative concerns."

Chapter II

"In a rather grand manner," Bingley said pointedly.

This Darcy could not dispute. "True enough. We certainly make no secret of our standing, but who does? I am not saying that one should not live up to one's condition, only that one must not ever lose sight of one's expenses. Why take a property that cannot support itself when there are so many that will?"

"We do not *know* that Netherfield cannot pay for itself."

"The point is, you did not bother to enquire into the matter. You never look before you leap. That you usually land on your feet is purest luck, and no man can afford to run his affairs in that manner. And I mean affairs in both senses of the word." Darcy arched his brow at Bingley.

"You must forgive me, Darcy," said Bingley with evident sincerity. "I fail to take your meaning."

"Bingley, do you mean to tell me that you are unaware of the speculations — nay, the expectations — you gave rise to amongst Miss Grantley's friends last June? Surely you must be aware that all of Society had marked you off the list of marriageable men on the strength of your obvious regard for her."

"I *was* rather partial to her," Bingley admitted.

"Partial! I should say! You had even *me* wondering."

"Darcy, you cannot suppose there was any impropriety in my actions, nor in my intentions," Bingley said in an injured tone. "I never even hinted at an offer; nor were we ever alone, or close to it!"

"My dear man, I should never dispute your integrity, nor your intentions; I know you. Your honour and character are beyond reproach. It was only that you spent so much time in her company and were so unguarded in your partiality that any one looking on would naturally assume an understanding existed between you."

"But I liked her," Bingley said with simple innocence.

"And she liked you, I am sure. But this is London, and Society is a jungle where bachelors are legitimate prey. It is the duty of every woman of standing to procure an advantageous marriage. Do but consider that in showing so marked a preference you were, in effect, keeping her from her duty; while you occupied her attentions, she could not turn them to another, more profitable line."

"I never thought of it that way," Bingley said. "I say, that's a rather unromantic way of seeing things, Darcy." He studied his friend silently for a moment. "I cannot say I like looking at it that way."

"I cannot say I do either," Darcy agreed with a tinge of bitterness. "But there it is: life is what it is, and our wishes will not change it."

"But Darcy, marriage must be more than a business venture, surely! From what you have told me, your own parents' marriage *proves* that it can be otherwise."

Darcy sat back. His parents were now both dead, his mother over eight years and his father five; he remembered them with a pain of loss undimmed by the passage of years. They had indeed seemed to enjoy that felicity and sublime unity of spirit one hoped for in one's married life. Yet....

"Does it? Does it, truly?" Darcy mused, slowly pushing his food about on his plate. "My mother was the eldest daughter of the Earl of Andover; she married into the Darcys — hardly what you would call an imprudent love match. The fact that they were happy together is, I am forced to conclude, happenstance; merely one of those rare sports sent down by Heaven to plague us with a vision of perfection that none of us can ever hope to realise." His own profitless Season and Georgiana's broken heart were much in his thoughts as he spoke.

"That is rather hard," said Bingley in protest. "A bleak prospect for the rest of us, I must say, if that be the case."

"How many of your married acquaintances would you say were happy?" Darcy challenged him. "The Hursts? Your own parents? Any one in your entire acquaintance?"

"The Hursts! I cannot think what Louisa was about when she accepted him. And my parents.... Well, my father was always so busy, you know, and Mater..." Bingley broke off with a rather embarrassed air.

Chapter II

"Just so. It is the same with me: I cannot think of any one outside my parents whose nuptials did not signal a very decided decrease in their happiness. By simple observation we must conclude that this is the rule, not the exception."

Bingley shook his head. "However sound your logic might be, I refuse to accept your conclusion; it *does* happen. And as long as a marriage such as your parents' *can* happen, why should it not happen to us? No, Darcy—as long as there *is* hope, I *will* hope."

Darcy slowly gave half a nod and said, "You are right, of course, Bingley. One can always hope—no matter how dismal the prospects seem." His air was even less optimistic than his words.

Bingley made an attempt to lift his spirits. "Speaking of hope, let us entertain some hopes for this Tuesday's dance: who can say but what we will meet the companions of our future lives that very night?"

"My dear Bingley, what can you be thinking of! What ladies of any consequence, save your own sisters, do you suppose might attend a country assembly in a three-by-four market-town?"

"What does consequence have to do with it?"

"You were speaking of hope, were you not? If you did not mean the hope of finding a suitable young woman of good standing, I quite mistook your meaning."

"Well...yes, of course. But gentlemen's daughters are to be found in the country, I assure you."

"None likely to suit. Now really, Bingley, would your family countenance a girl without a fortune to do justice to your family's position?"

"If she were sweet enough, I am sure they would."

"Are you, really? I do not think I could say the same."

"Darcy! Would you truly form an attachment for purely mercenary reasons?"

"I should not *choose* to do so; but if the women of Society have an obligation, so do we men: marry well and secure the line. Form an attachment? Perhaps not, but it

Into Hertfordshire

does not follow that there can be no marriage where there is no attachment." That Darcy's words were meant in all sincerity might be argued, but last winter's Season had indeed been bleak.

Bingley was clearly shocked. "I cannot believe you really mean that, Darcy."

Darcy stared over his friend's shoulder for a moment before drawing a sigh. "Well, perhaps I do not," he admitted in a conciliatory manner. "I do not wish it so, but look around you, man! I have been at this game longer than you have, and, whilst I do not pretend to plough the ground quite so rapidly as you do, I *have* covered the territory—last winter was my ninth Season, after all. Yet whom have you ever met who you would seriously consider offering for?"

"No one. But all the more reason to broaden the search. And I say, let us begin in Hertfordshire! I *will* have you come to the dance, Darcy!"

Darcy grimaced. "I really have no stomach for it, Bingley. Let your sister find a swain from among your new neighbours, I pray you. No doubt there will be many young men simply panting to make her acquaintance."

"I am thinking of you, Darcy, not my sister. I cannot abide seeing you give way to such feelings. It is not you. I know it is not." Having stepped thus far beyond the bounds of masculine decorum, he quickly shifted his ground, saying, "Besides, I have already told Caroline you were to attend. She is doubtless choosing her gown at this very moment."

"No, Bingley, I was too hasty. I do not wish it. I dislike dancing. I always feel such an object! Being sensible of the girl's expectations and hopes; being stared at by her mamma—not to mention the rest of the company, all the cats behind their fans; no—I shall stay at home and be at ease."

"You dislike dancing so much because you have never had a partner you were partial to, that is all." Darcy shook his head without speaking, and Bingley switched back to his strong suit: "Truly, though, it would be awkward for Caroline to have no partner in the beginning; makes her

Chapter II

look a bit undesirable, does not it? She would not care for it, and neither should I, if it comes to that. She would not go, and I really could not blame her. Then how should we appear to those Country gentry you speak so feelingly of?"

Darcy sighed heavily and reluctantly conceded: "I would not deny your sister the opportunity to establish herself properly in the neighbourhood."

"Excellent! Done, then," said Bingley, fairly pouncing on Darcy's words. "She will be most pleased."

"Yes, quite," said Darcy dryly. "But let us have a right understanding; I shall squire her into the room, and I shall dance one dance with her, but that is my uttermost limit. No doubt she will establish herself as queen of the ball without any further assistance from me, and I have no inclination to make a display of myself amongst strangers."

"Display!" scoffed Bingley. "How, precisely, can dancing at a ball be translated into making a display of oneself? Every one does so at a ball; that is its purpose, after all."

"Not for me, I assure you. I have never in seven-and-twenty years managed to get through a dance with any degree of pleasure, and I cannot imagine that I shall learn differently in the five days before your assembly."

"You, Sir, are impossible. I…"

"Bingley, leave off! You have taken your point: I shall go to your wretched dance. But do not imagine that I go to find enjoyment, much less my future wife."

"Yes, but Darcy…" Bingley started persuasively.

"Desist, Sir!" Darcy drew himself up in his chair until Bingley's eyes were level with his chin and favoured him with his fiercest scowl. Since he topped Bingley by a good six inches and was commensurately broad across the shoulders, he made a fine, imposing figure of a man.

"All right! Quarter — I cry quarter!" said Bingley half laughing, half serious. "Calm yourself. Here, have some wine, eat something; your dinner is getting cold. Upon my word, I never met any one who could work himself up the way you do, Darcy. Good Lord, I hardly know but what I should have fared better at home with Caroline."

Into Hertfordshire

Darcy's ire deflated instantly in the face of his friend's tolerant good humour. He stared at his plate for a moment and said, "I beg your pardon, Charles, most sincerely. My deuced temper…inexcusable. Pax, old man?"

"Pax," agreed Bingley easily.

"I fear my zeal for winning my point sometimes amounts to a mania; it must expose my friends to a degree of insolence it quite shames me to realise. I cannot think where I acquired such a dreadful habit. If ever I repeat this performance I give you leave to call me on the carpet directly. Agreed?"

"Do not give it a thought," Bingley pardoned him with the goodness and charity that was a primary source of Darcy's regard for him. "For the most part the points you make are good ones; you talk better sense than any one else in my acquaintance — of course, my acquaintance does include my sisters and their friends."

In spite of his friend's easy acquittal, Darcy still felt contrite; his temper had always been his weakness; when it got the upper hand he always regretted it. He firmly believed in proper behaviour: that, no matter the occasion, one's civility should never desert one; moreover, that the more one wished to show one's regard, the more strictly one must adhere to the tenets of decorum. As a child he had been taught that proper behaviour was good behaviour, and he had never learnt to feel differently. His standards of conduct were higher than most, and tended to make him appear rather more formal than was common. He did make a distinction between those closest to him and the rest of the world, naturally, and when closeted with his intimates he did loosen his tight grip on his manners, as any one might do; but in company he was unvaryingly correct. This had earned him a reputation for reserve which was not entirely deserved; he was, in fact, a reasonably affable man whose faith in proper comportment, as a symbol of his gentlemanly regard for what was due his fellow creatures, manifested itself in an exacting observance of propriety. The fact that Bingley's very opposite views seemed to give him and all of

Chapter II

his acquaintance the greatest pleasure, and surrounded him with many well-wishers, did not appear to influence Darcy's prejudices in the slightest.

Darcy's contrition carried him through the rest of the evening. He was so obliging and agreeable in trying to make up for his lapse in manners that the two friends parted on the best of terms.

Chapter Three

*D*arcy would have leisure to regret being quite so obliging on the morrow, for he had agreed to travel with Bingley and his sister in their coach, rather than take his own. Miss Bingley was strongly persuaded that Darcy was to be the font of her future felicity, and this persuasion made itself felt to the fullest that day. As she sat across from him she constantly sought his eye with hers, begged to have his observations on the passing scenery, presumed his agreement with her observations on the same, and availed herself of his person for support whenever the coach lurched heavily enough to give her a plausible excuse. And for the four hours of the journey she blithely ignored his marked lack of enthusiasm for the conversation. Bingley contented himself with avoiding Darcy's eye and pretending to doze as much as possible; thus was he gently avenged for his trials at his friend's hands the night before.

The Hursts followed behind in a chaise, with the gentlemen's hunters behind. Mrs. Louisa Hurst, Bingley's eldest sister, was a woman of limited understanding, whose chief interest lay in seconding her sister Caroline's opinions and echoing her least observations with an enthusiasm they rarely merited. Nor was Mr. Hurst Darcy's sort; just one of hundreds of London gentlemen with neither occupation nor desire for one. His one social attainment was a proficiency at cards, which made him a tolerable companion to Darcy, he being fond of that pastime.

Darcy's enthusiasm for the trip began to revive as they entered the environs of Netherfield Park, for he was generally pleased with what he saw. The farmland was well laid out; the soil, dark and rich, was to be seen between the stalks left behind by the harvest; sheaves of forage were

Chapter III

being tied in neat bundles by workers here and there, putting the fields in order for the winter.

Bingley's first true moment of triumph occurred just after they passed the gates into the park. A superb stand of shaggy timber extended away towards the left from the gates, and just outside its borders they surprised a herd of a dozen deer, led by a magnificent buck, whose snort of alarm sent the herd bounding for the trees. He momentarily favoured the coach with a wary regard before bounding away himself to join his charges. Bingley caught Darcy's eye and both men smiled, appreciating the prospect of an exceptional hunt.

"Fine animal, that," murmured Darcy.

"Looked well-fed, did not they?" agreed Bingley. "The lands hereabout must be remarkably fertile," he added with a challenging smile at Darcy.

That gentleman gave his own snort in reply. "That, or your landlord could not afford to hire a gamekeeper to chase the beasts out of the corn," he said.

Bingley grinned and shook his head at his friend's obstinacy.

The approach to the Hall was quite fine, although for Darcy, accustomed as he was to Pemberley's magnificence, it had not the effect it might otherwise have had. Still, he found nothing to criticise, and even some things to admire. Bingley's smile of pleasure grew in proportion to Darcy's appreciative comments.

"Do you truly like it?" Bingley enquired at last. His sister stilled her own comment and awaited Darcy's eagerly.

"It is splendid, Bingley, indeed," Darcy said. "Of course, until we ride the whole of it, it is hard to say with certainty, but I should say that every thing we have seen augurs well for the place."

Bingley's chest lifted at this rare compliment and Miss Bingley sat back with a satisfied expression. "It is well, then," said Bingley. "We will settle in this afternoon, and I told Roberts to have a late welcoming dinner ready for seven o'clock. To-morrow we can take to horse and make the grand tour."

This happy plan met with general approbation, and the various members of the party dispersed to their respective apartments. The manor house was modern and well-appointed, and even Mr. Hurst, who was an indolent man given to airs of wealth and discrimination which he did not, in fact, possess, found nought to criticise for his evening's comforts.

The next morning Darcy awoke in the grey before dawn, owing to an unfamiliar bed and a window sash that rattled in a breeze that was just beginning to rise. Even as he turned over and buried his head in the pillow he knew it was hopeless: he was awake for the day, for good or ill. He pushed himself out of bed without much enthusiasm, knowing he had a full and very long day ahead of him. Bingley's new housemaids were already at their work, for the fire in his dressing-room was ablaze. He began his morning ablutions without bothering to ring for his man, with the charitable thought of allowing at least that member of the entourage a bit more rest.

He had nearly managed to finish dressing before that worthy appeared. "Mr. Darcy, Sir! Why did not you ring? I had no thought but I would find you still a-bed!"

"I woke early, Perkins, and saw no need for you to lose sleep as well. But as you are here, see what you can do with this infernal neck cloth. It does not want to behave itself this morning."

"Yes, Sir. Let me just have a look." He took the offending article of clothing out of his master's hand. "The cook here knows his business, Sir; Nicholls is his name. Your coffee should be ready now, and breakfast at our usual time, Sir."

Perkins had been with Darcy since his university days. He was several years younger than his master and had first come to the Darcy household as a footman under Darcy's father. He had had the best upbringing and education that his father, a tenant farmer on the Darcy estates, could give

Chapter III

him, and he was a naturally civil and politic individual. About the time that Darcy was preparing to leave for Oxford there had been a fire in the stables: a cat had tipped a lantern off a shelf. Perkins had distinguished himself during this crisis, repeatedly entering the building to rescue his master's stock and belongings at serious risk of injury to himself. This distinction had been suitably rewarded by his elevation to valet to the master's son. He took his duties seriously, and was given to studying those matters of fashion to which his master did not deign to give his attention.

His neck cloth arranged to Perkins' satisfaction, Darcy said, "Very good. Do I look all right?"

"Very fine, Mr. Darcy. And you'll have a lovely day for your ride." He paused and looked up at his master. "I did, hear, Sir…"

"Go on, Perkins. What have you discovered now?" asked Darcy. His manservant had the habit of bringing to his master's attention any intelligence he had gleaned below stairs.

"Well, Sir, Mr. Hurst will not be joining you this morning, as he is unwell. He had perhaps a bit more of the grain than he ought last night, and is not likely to appear before noon."

Darcy scoffed. "He never will learn not to wrestle with John Barleycorn. Well, that is no great loss. Aught else?"

"No, Sir, except that Miss Bingley's maid did say her mistress was rather put out that you gentlemen were planning to be out all day."

"Miss Bingley…hmm. Thank you, Perkins." Man and master, while not given to sharing their opinions directly, understood each other; there was considerable similarity in their respective opinions of Mr. Bingley's younger sister, although they were each too well-mannered to mention it.

While Darcy was at first inclined to discount Miss Bingley's complaint as no more than her usual petulant desire to have her own way in all matters, a second thought revealed that this pattern was repeating itself with increasing regularity. It was clear she was beginning to feel a sense of possessiveness concerning himself and was, by her actions, attempting to inflict this opinion upon him by the simple expedient of assuming the rights of ownership. There are, no doubt, men in the world who might be annexed merely by the exercise of such an assumption, but Darcy did not count himself among them, and resented both the presumption and the guile that Miss Bingley's actions exposed. Indeed, guile was one of his greatest irritants, and its constant use—nay, its nearly universal veneration—by the *ton* was at the heart of his deepest disapprobation of that set. Such were his thoughts as he descended to the breakfast-room some time later, where he immediately found a measure of support for his conclusions concerning Miss Bingley.

"Mr. Darcy!" Miss Bingley's voice greeted him. "Here you are! Your coffee is ready and I have sent down for your eggs-and-bacon." Her welcoming smile was smug and hinted at a degree of intimacy Darcy had not the least intention of encouraging.

"Good morning, Miss Bingley. I thank you, but I fancy a chop this morning. And I see fresh scones; that will suit me admirably." Her pretty little pout was lost on Darcy, who had turned away to the side table to get his coffee and butter a scone. He generally did prefer eggs-and-bacon, but a chop was a small sacrifice to maintain the proper distance between himself and Miss Bingley.

Bingley and Mrs. Hurst soon joined the party, and the discussion among the four of them revolved around the two topics of the day's tour and the night's entertainment. The women's partiality for the latter soon drove the men out of doors to pursue the former, and they found there a very beautiful autumn morning in full progress. Darcy's hunter, a fine and spirited animal, was restive after his time in the London stables; Darcy had his hands full until the two friends indulged in a race which brought workers up from their tasks and more than one admiring shout. Not knowing the land, they kept to the lanes and let the horses have their heads. They ran at a full gallop for at least a mile and a half

Chapter III

through the quiet back lanes between Netherfield and Meryton, until the horses were thoroughly winded, their breath blowing great puffs of steam into the chill of the morning. This knocked the devils out of them and the two men, laughing and exhilarated, were able to proceed with their investigations without further difficulty.

They returned to the Hall late in the morning for a cup of tea, for the day remained cold, and then went right out again. Over the course of the next several hours they identified a very considerable number of repairs and improvements needed to bring the property up to its full potential, but even Darcy was forced to admit that the land was good, and the current uses well organised and thought out. He would not venture to pronounce it worthy of purchase until they had reviewed the books for the past four or five years, but allowed that it looked hopeful. Bingley, according to his nature, was for ever falling into raptures over possible hunting courses, the picturesque of vantage points, and plans for follies, fountains, waterfalls, dams for duck ponds, and all such manner of extravagant and unnecessary additions to the beauties Nature had amply provided.

They finally finished their ramblings in the late afternoon. Returning to the Hall, Bingley wanted to go straight to the salon and send for refreshments, as dinner had been early that day in consequence of the evening's outing, but Darcy protested that they had too much of horseflesh about them and insisted that he, at least, would go up for a change of clothes before meeting the ladies.

Going up stairs, he found Perkins in his chambers, busily laying out things for the evening; hardly a single horizontal surface in his dressing-room was left uncovered. While Perkins helped him to change for the drawing-room, Darcy enquired after the state of disarray. "Are we in search of something particular, Perkins? You seem to have laid out every stitch of evening clothes we brought."

"Yes, Sir. Miss Bingley sent her maid to me, Sir, while you were out. She gave me the particulars of Miss Bingley's

Into Hertfordshire

dress for the evening in order that your attire might complement hers, Sir."

"I *beg* your pardon?" demanded Darcy.

"Yes, Sir," replied Perkins, his manner conveying that his opinion of the matter entirely coincided with that of his master.

That gentleman was highly incensed. The brass! It was one thing to send to ask what one might intend to wear so that she might alter her choice to match, but to issue *instructions*! Before Darcy could find words to express his feelings, Perkins hastened to explain his activities. "Not knowing, Sir, how best to manage, I thought it as well to give you a selection. These," he pointed to one grouping, "will match with the lady's dress admirably, while those," and here he pointed to another group, "will neither make nor mar her looks. But these," and here he pointed with a hint of a flourish, "will quarrel so with her gown that no one could bear looking at the two of you together." He was too well schooled to so much as smile, but there was an impish twinkle in his eye.

"Ah, Perkins," grinned Darcy, "what a lovely thought." He looked down a second time and the smile became a chuckle. "I shall have to think it over, but I appreciate your thoroughness and, all things considered, propriety."

"Yes, Sir. Thank you, Sir."

Although Darcy was still chuckling as he went downstairs, he by no means forgot to be annoyed with Miss Bingley. Blast a woman, anyhow! Having granted her a degree of familiarity, he recognised the necessity of certain concessions contrary to his customary activities, but this was becoming intolerable. Yet, constantly thrown together as they were, he could not very well be consistently disobliging to her without creating hardship for Bingley. How could he control her rampant attempts to engage his interest without injury to his friend? It was precisely the sort of dilemma that resulted from those drawing-room intrigues so beloved by Society misses, and so despised by Darcy.

Chapter III

Thus, it was with a decidedly martial spirit that Darcy entered the salon. Bingley and the rest of the party were already there. Bracing himself to meet with more impertinence from Miss Bingley, he sat down. But her first observation was directed, not at him, but at her brother. "There, Charles, this is a true gentleman. He is but a very few minutes behind you, yet he is suitably attired for the salon, instead of the stables."

"I was hungry, Caroline!" Bingley protested.

"I dare say Mr. Darcy was too, yet he could control those urgings we share with the rest of God's creatures long enough to present a civilised appearance. A man, however pleasant his character, must always endeavour to overcome his animal nature."

Darcy could find nothing in this speech to which he could take exception. Indeed, he had to admit to himself that he quite agreed.

Not so with Bingley. "'Animal nature', Caroline!" he expostulated. "You make it sound as if I were a ravening beast, when all I have done is to sit here quietly in the most composed manner and eat a piece of cake."

"Well, you certainly smell like a beast," said his sister with a disdainful sniff.

"I pray you, Darcy, support me here," he implored his friend.

"Readily, Sir, but for one, small, inconsequential detail."

"Which is?"

"Your sister is right."

Throwing up his hands, Bingley rose and fetched himself more cake from the sideboard. Then he sat himself down at the greatest possible distance from the table. "There! Now no one need be troubled by my savage ravening or my bestial stench."

During the rest of the afternoon Miss Bingley, being engaged with her sister on some needlework, had little to say, save to enquire once in a demur manner if Darcy required anything. Therefore, as Darcy ascended to his

Into Hertfordshire

apartment he found himself in rather greater charity with her than when he had descended. Had he been the truly rational creature he wished to be, he would have seen that Miss Bingley's impertinence had merely been directed at an object other than himself, and resented it with equal intensity. But since he agreed with her, her expression of distaste seemed to him only good sense, and he quite overlooked the fact that, as a younger sister and an unmarried woman, the dictates of civilised behaviour she so highly esteemed gave her no right to criticise her older brother at all.

Darcy's selection for his evening attire was that of the neutral grouping, although he looked appreciatively at those quarrelsome garments lying so temptingly to one side. When Perkins had got him to the stage where there was little more to do than don his coat, a strong fit of lassitude overcame him, as the short night and long day's activities worked on him. He sat down heavily and looked longingly at his bed.

"Perkins, I have a mind to lie down for a bit."

"Sir!" his man protested, "you would be all over wrinkles!"

"It is only a country assembly, man, not St. James'."

"All the more reason, Sir!" Perkins' tone momentarily took on the admonitory accents of injured propriety. This was quickly subdued, however, and he explained with dignity, "If you were to turn out at court with wrinkles it would be a mark of distinction, owing either to some great need or to your disdain of convention. But here in the country, Sir, wrinkles are common, in both senses of the word. Why, it would be as much as my place is worth if I was to let you go out so; I could never hold my head up again below stairs. Let me go fetch you a cup of tea, instead, Sir."

"You had better make it coffee, Perkins; I fear tea would be insufficient to the task."

As Darcy sat waiting for his man to return, he sank into a brown study as the day's bustle dropt from him, leaving him enervated and stupid. His thoughts began drifting; they first stopped on Georgiana. He had had no

Chapter III

letter from her for nearly a fortnight, which was unusual and troubling. Her last had been troubling, too: merely a recitation of her reading and musical studies, it was more like a journal entry than a letter from his closest relation. The woman he had engaged as her companion sent him weekly reports which assured him that his sister was not unwell, but still.... He dwelt on this for a time, feeling how wrong it was for him to be frivoling here in the hinterlands when she needed his care; but then she had practically begged him to go back to London that she might have whatever comfort she could find in solitude. From there his thoughts drifted to Wickham: how dearly he would like to visit some great ruin on that man—no, not a man; a monster. Nothing could be too horrible for a creature like Wickham. If only this were an hundred years earlier, when the laws of society were bent more in favour of the *victims* of such acts as Wickham's, rather than treating them as though they themselves were the villains...society: hmmph! Society, indeed! Society and all its nattering, idle, venal women; untouched by cares themselves, they could feel nothing for the cares of others. Georgiana's inconsolable pain would have been nothing more than a delectable morsel of gossip for them. Scavengers and carrion-feeders, all of them. His imagination brought them instantly before him, gasping and tittering behind their fans at the scandal, their eyes watching him every where but never meeting his own; whispering, passing secretive little notes.... Why had not Georgiana written? She never went more than two or three days without writing.... He should be at Pemberley looking after her, not wasting his time amongst the unlettered and unwashed at a country dance.... Dancing, what a foolish waste of human energies....

His thoughts continued in this slow revolve until Perkins arrived with a cup of strong, black coffee and a covered tray. "I took it upon me to bring you a bite of food too, Sir. The 'refreshments' at the assembly might not live up to the name, Sir, if you take my meaning."

33

Into Hertfordshire

"Ah, Perkins, that was well thought of." Darcy roused himself and went to the small table near the window. The sun was just setting, and the sky was sharp and clear. The night will be cold, he thought with a sort of bleak satisfaction.

Chapter Four

*D*arcy was the first one downstairs. This was not unusual—rather the opposite—so he was by no means surprised, but still it annoyed him that no one in Bingley's entire household could contrive to be on time. Next to arrive were Miss Bingley and Mrs. Hurst, and as they descended the stairs they were the picture of Darcy's Society women; their fans aflutter, giggling and whispering, they were the very creatures of his imagination, and unconsciously drew his resentment down upon themselves. Miss Bingley came up to him, her smiles fading. She viewed his attire with a quizzical look. Her gown was of lively colours; his own stark black and white, as Perkins had predicted, added nothing to her appearance, though it did not contrast with it. Darcy thought with some satisfaction of the "quarrelsome" grouping: it would indeed have made her look a scarecrow.

"How...striking...you look this evening, Mr. Darcy," she drawled, stepping back from him, her lips drawn into a thin line of dissatisfaction. "Your man has turned you out most carefully."

"I thank you, Miss Bingley," he replied. Since her own compliment was patently insincere, he did not feel compelled to offer one in return. As the silence lengthened between them, her eyes flashed and she turned back to her sister with a toss of her head. Darcy was thus left in the full enjoyment of a marked contempt for them both, and, indeed, the society of all women. When Hurst and Bingley came down, the party went out to the carriages. Miss Bingley very pointedly entered her brother-in-law's carriage, leaving Darcy and Bingley to themselves in Bingley's coach. Darcy could not be sorry for the fact, but her obvious disdain did little to appease his mood.

Into Hertfordshire

Bingley was in high spirits, and Darcy was in a frame of mind to be offended even by the heedless cheer of his friend. He knew from experience that Bingley would enjoy himself to the hilt, would immediately and effortlessly become familiar with the entire company, would draw the prettiest woman exclusively to himself for a dancing partner, and would very soon develop a discernible partiality towards her. How he contrived all this in the space of a single evening was beyond Darcy's understanding, but he had seen it often enough to be convinced of the inexorable nature of the proceedings.

At length Bingley became aware of his friend's withdrawn attitude and asked whether he was quite himself. Darcy made but small reply and Bingley looked at him with concern. He spent the rest of the short trip attempting to brighten Darcy's mood, but to little effect.

Bingley himself brightened again when they arrived at the edge of the little town of Meryton. The faint strains of a lively air reached their ears. "There, Darcy, you shall see: I am sure we shall enjoy the evening. And who knows? — that certain she might well be within." Darcy gave a listless snort in reply. They pulled up in front of the hall and descended. Darcy brought himself to his full height, squared his shoulders like Guy Fawkes about to mount the hangman's scaffold, and turned to escort Miss Bingley into the assembly.

The appearance of the newcomers naturally caused a stir and a wave of whispers to spread through the room. And certainly Darcy, given his stature, his fashionable attire, and well-featured face, received his full share of the attention. Unfortunately, that very attention, which for most persons would have been a welcome sign of consequence and notice, served to fix in him the dark mood he had carried in with him; he felt like a caged bear being paraded at a country fair for the peasantry to gawk at. And, even more regrettably, the scrutiny he received created among the revellers a general awareness of his marked lack of enthusiasm for his surroundings; this was soon interpreted as scorn for

Chapter IV

the company in which he found himself. Such was his mood that when the early smiles and flutterings turned to blank stares and cold shoulders, it brought him, not a sense of his wrong-doing, but a perverse sense of vindication. That they should dislike him was proof of his acuity and insight. Society was the same every where, thought he with some bitterness; well enough, let the cats say what they would—it mattered little. Here, at least, he was not compelled to cater to it. He would never see any of them again in his life, so what did it signify? He was vaguely aware that he was behaving churlishly, and the better part of him felt it, but not so strongly that he was minded to break from the manner of his beginning.

While his friend was dancing, Darcy spent most of his time drifting about the room, having been introduced only to the family of one Sir William Lucas, whose conversation he found less than captivating. Under the circumstances, his strict sense of propriety would not allow him to enter into conversation with the others attending—even if he had had a desire to. But he was aware that his neighbours at the assembly looked at him with little approbation, and he allowed his sentiments to mirror theirs, leaving him with little reason to seek acquaintance with any of them. He watched with scant enthusiasm as his friend led his third, or possibly his fourth, partner down the dance, while he was left to amuse himself. Looking about the room he saw a number of young ladies without partners, and more than one whose countenance would satisfy all but the most exacting critics of female beauty; but in Darcy's present state of mind, their presence served only to remind him of how ill-suited he was to his surroundings: while he might in certain circumstances find himself able to enjoy their company, these were decidedly not such circumstances. The truth of the matter, not often admitted even to himself, was that Mr. Darcy was slow to feel comfortable with new people, and the force of will it would take on this occasion, to seek introduction and enter into conversation with a strange young woman, was simply not within his compass this

Into Hertfordshire

evening. Nor did he wish to converse with either of Bingley's sisters, given how things stood, and so he was left with no alternative but to simply wander about the place, trying to stay out of people's way, and, quite irrationally, becoming more and more provoked by the situation. At length Bingley left the dance to fetch his partner of the moment a refreshment, and found Darcy standing near the table of drinks. He took the opportunity to persuade his friend to enter into the spirit of the evening: "Come, Darcy, I must have you dance. I hate to see you standing about by yourself in this stupid manner. You had much better dance."

"I certainly shall not," replied Darcy irritably. Here Bingley had left him to his own devices for well over an hour, and now spoke to him only in passing—and to persuade him to dance, of all things. His glance travelled around the room, seeing again the same collection of strangers' faces; not a few of them turned coldly away from his gaze. "You know how I detest it, unless I am particularly acquainted with my partner. At such an assembly as this it would be insupportable. Your sisters are engaged, and there is not another woman in the room whom it would not be a punishment to me to stand up with."

"I would not be so fastidious as you are for a kingdom!" cried his friend. "Upon my honour, I never met with so many pleasant girls in my life as I have this evening; and there are several of them you see uncommonly pretty."

"*You* are dancing with the only handsome girl in the room." said Darcy, though this was certainly untrue; Bingley was merely dancing with the *most* handsome girl in the room. But his present mood was such that Darcy was ready to disagree on any and every point.

"Oh! She is the most beautiful creature I ever beheld!" exclaimed Bingley. "But there is one of her sisters sitting down just behind you, who is very pretty, and I dare say very agreeable. Do let me ask my partner to introduce you."

"Which do you mean?" He turned around and saw a young woman seated nearby, happily engaged in watching

Chapter IV

the dance. He had noticed her earlier, and had resisted the inclination to let his eye linger in her direction more than once during his wanderings, but he would by no means admit as much to Bingley. Her dark eyes, alive with mirth and yet at the same time showing an astute appreciation of all that was passing, had caught his attention particularly. Now, sensing his observation of her, she turned to meet his gaze. Not wishing to see her eyes harden as she recognised who it was that beheld her, or perhaps because his more gentlemanly side felt his general incivility during the evening, he quickly withdrew his own glance. To Bingley he said, "She is tolerable, but not handsome enough to tempt *me*. I am in no humour at present to give consequence to young ladies who are slighted by other men. You had better return to your partner and enjoy her smiles, for you are wasting your time with me." Bingley left him with a smile and a shrug of the shoulders. Darcy then glanced cautiously back over his shoulder for fear he might have been overheard; but the young woman had turned away and did not appear to have paid them any attention. He was relieved: ill-humour he would allow himself—open discourtesy he would not. However, had he been able to observe her while he was speaking, he would have seen the young lady's eyes widen at his ill-mannered and disobliging description of herself.

Darcy held true to his course for the rest of the evening, dancing only one set each with Mrs. Hurst and Miss Bingley, having promised Bingley he would do so, and waited out his delivery from durance. At length the musicians, yawning and stretching themselves, packed up their instruments, forcing Bingley at last to stop dancing. The Netherfield party returned to their carriages in nearly universal good spirits; the ladies were tired but smiling, and every one save Darcy had enjoyed themselves—after their fashion. Bingley and Darcy helped Hurst stagger into his carriage and handed his lady in beside him. He was snoring contentedly before they had closed the door.

Into Hertfordshire

On her part, Miss Bingley was well pleased with her social conquests: introductions to her were much sought after, as was her hand for the dancing. She was sufficiently mollified to condescend to enter her brother's coach with good grace for the ride home. He congratulated her on her success: "Well, Caroline, you must be pleased; you might have danced every dance, had you wished it." Such was his view of things that to be sought after for dancing was of greater import than being deferred to by one's new acquaintances. Not so his sister. She was secretly delighted by her new-found status, but could scarcely say as much; to have made a conquest among such a company was no great distinction, and to be pleased by it was therefore beneath her dignity.

"The dancing was, indeed, the best part of the evening: at least the music was well played," she sniffed. "Certainly the people themselves had little to offer."

"Caroline, how can you speak so?" demanded Bingley. "Our new neighbours are as a fine a set of people as any one could wish to meet — most accommodating. Every one wanted to make your acquaintance."

"Yes, Charles, but that is more than I can say in return. Who would wish to be acquainted with such people? No fashion, no taste, no conversation; no — I can take no pleasure in being esteemed by such as these. Do not you agree, Mr. Darcy?" She looked at Darcy, certain of the coincidence of their feelings on this point, at least.

"Indeed. I have never spent a more pointless evening."

"How the two of you can come away from such an evening as this without having received a jot of pleasure is beyond me," cried Bingley. "Every one was most kind, and seemed sincere in their desire to be so. And I have never been in company with such a collection of pretty girls in all my life."

"Oh, Charles!" exclaimed Miss Bingley, "a fine countenance is every virtue in your eyes."

Bingley gave his sister a cool look. "I am not so callow as you make out, Caroline. But I defy you to find fault with

Chapter IV

Miss Bennet," he said, naming the partner he favoured most during the evening.

"Oh! There, Charles, I quite agree with you. She *is* a sweet girl. I should not mind knowing her better."

"Do not you agree, Darcy?" Bingley asked.

"She is handsome," he allowed, but he could not leave the compliment unalloyed, "To my taste, however, she smiles too much."

Bingley laughed at his friend. "There is just no pleasing you to-night, Darcy. 'Smiles too much', indeed. How absurd!"

As Darcy prepared for sleep that evening, he could not help but hear Bingley's words echo in his mind. He felt that he *had* acted absurdly, and part of him wished he had shown better manners. But another part of him felt that a goodly portion of the blame for his behaviour, if not all, most properly belonged to the people with whom he was forced to consort. Whether in Town or Country, Society played the same games and with the same lack of substance. Vapid and vacuous, not all their fine trappings could disguise their lack of true depth and delicacy of feeling. His only wish was never to be in company with this present lot again.

His ill-tempered fault-finding carried him to bed. Just as he was dropping off to sleep, though, the vision of a dark-eyed face, lovely and alive with pleasure, came unbidden to his mind.

Chapter Five

*T*o Darcy's misfortune, his hope and his prophecy of never seeing any members of the assembly again, was not to be borne out. Three days after the dance, the ladies of one of the principal families of the neighbourhood came to visit the ladies of Netherfield. This was the Bennet family, and amongst them was Mr. Bingley's partner from the dance, Miss Jane Bennet; she brought with her her mother and four sisters. Darcy therefore found himself, and with some discomposure, in company again with the young woman whom he had slighted to Bingley. She appeared to even greater advantage in the full light, and her voice was a pleasant, warm contralto. Darcy, however, was able to appreciate neither her looks, her tone, nor her company. As his mood had passed, her pleasing manners, composure, and fine countenance gave him to feel all the discourtesy he had been guilty of at the assembly; this left him awkward in her presence, and, as awkwardness was nearly unknown to him, he unconsciously turned his disapprobation on the person who caused it. The young lady, Miss Elizabeth Bennet, gave no indication that she remembered his behaviour at the dance with any disfavour; indeed, she seemed hardly aware that he had been at the assembly at all. Nor, it seemed, did his presence at this meeting impress her to any degree: she barely glanced at him after the introductions were made. This was a novelty to him; as Darcy of Pemberley he was used to being the cynosure of young women's attention on first acquaintance; Miss Elizabeth Bennet was no more interested in him than if he had been the baker's son. He shrugged inwardly and determined to answer her indifference with his own.

Bingley, of course, was delighted to see his dancing partner again. Miss Jane Bennet was the eldest of the Miss

Chapter V

Bennets. She, too, appeared to advantage in the daytime, and her smiles were just as prevalent as before, although there was also an undeniable sincerity and sweetness about her. Darcy saw with tolerant amusement that his friend was well on his way to being in love again. Bingley danced attendance on her like the Earth around the Sun. There were three other Bennet daughters, as well: younger, less well-featured, less well-mannered, and a great deal less worthy of notice. The two youngest, especially, seemed scarcely more than children; Darcy wondered at their being out in Society at such a young age. After half-an-hour in their company, he heartily wished that they were not.

But if the youngest were immodest and impertinent, the mother strained the bounds of credulity; surely Darcy had never met any one with such a wonderful lack of understanding. If mention was made of some event of the day, she was sure to be ignorant of it; if some one essayed a witticism, she was sure to miss its meaning; it seemed almost as if she was engaging in an elaborate prank—no one could have an understanding so little developed. Her own conversation was composed of nothing but fulsome compliments for Bingley, his house, and his sisters, and thinly veiled attempts to assess the value of each and every article that passed beneath her eye. She fairly bubbled over with admiration for all that Bingley said and possessed; yet towards Darcy, she was markedly different: strangely abrupt and even cold. Given her conversational skills he felt his good fortune, but it was a curious circumstance. Her entire character was a puzzle, but not one Darcy felt any inclination to delve into.

When the Bennets left, Miss Bingley and Mrs. Hurst, as was their habit, proceeded to gleefully and mercilessly shred their new friends' characters, manners, dress, and wit. When they broached the subject of Miss Elizabeth Bennet, Miss Bingley said laughingly, "I was absolutely *non plus* when she was introduced to me at the assembly, for Sir William Lucas had mentioned her as one of the leading beauties of the neighbourhood. Upon my honour, I believed

Into Hertfordshire

him to have been making a jest at my expense, and I very nearly said so; but then he is not, perhaps, as we now know, the most discerning of men. What do you think, Mr. Darcy? Would you say Miss Elizabeth Bennet is a beauty worthy of note?"

Darcy, having been ignored by the lady in question, annoyed by her younger sisters, and quite astounded by her mother, revenged himself on them collectively by observing wryly: "She a beauty? I would sooner call her mother a wit." Miss Bingley laughed immoderately at this, as did her sister; even Hurst gave a chuckle and nod in Darcy's direction, which for him was unbridled hilarity.

Nevertheless, the ladies declared the two elder Bennet sisters to be worthy of a closer acquaintance, and therefore returned the visit two days later, on a dark, overcast Saturday morning. Longbourn, the estate of Mr. Bennet, was three miles distant on the other side of Meryton. The ladies were attended on this visit by their brother, who, as Darcy had foreseen almost from their first dance together, was much smitten by Miss Bennet. The excuse given by Bingley for his accompanying the ladies was the need to see how his coach performed in the weather after receiving some slight repairs in the village. To this Darcy offered no challenge, though the repairs had been complete for a week without Bingley expressing any interest in them; he knew full well why his friend wished to visit the Bennets. Darcy was unconcerned by this display of partiality, however, having seen it run its course in his friend before; he was also mindful of his trespass on Bingley's privileges only a fortnight prior, and therefore spoke no word of caution to his friend.

During the ensuing days, Darcy and Miss Elizabeth Bennet were thrown into each other's company several times. They dined together in company the Monday following their introduction at Netherfield, and now were met again on Wednesday evening at a large party. He had begun his observations of her when he was in a mood to be pleased by no one, and on a second viewing he yet remained proof against her charms, but by the third he found

Chapter V

himself following her every where with his eyes. He was forced to admit to himself that, while not at all fashionable, her clothes were well-suited to her figure; and that, even though he had withstood the allures of women whose features were unquestionably superior to hers, the expressiveness of her eyes and the pleasing curve of her mouth when she smiled caught his attention to an unprecedented degree. He admitted this to himself, however, only to the degree of congratulating himself on having found at least *one* point of moderate interest amongst his new acquaintance in Hertfordshire.

Their host of the evening on this, their fourth rencontre, Sir William Lucas, was a man whose fortune had been made in trade and whose elevation to rank had occurred some ten years prior. As a result of his late acquisition of a courtly title, Sir William was perhaps overly scrupulous in his observation of those courtesies he felt to be attendant on rank, from the desire to appear that he had held that privilege throughout the entirety of his life. Aside from this tendency he was an unassuming man, good-natured and desirous of seeing all around him comfortable and easy. He was therefore fond of entertainments, and, being as well pleased to give them as to attend them, was known throughout the neighbourhood as an excellent host.

The general conversation at Sir William's party was, to Darcy's mind, no more than what one would expect in the country: weather, roads, and stale gossip from London. With such a limited field for discourse of interest to himself, Darcy several times found opportunity to position himself at vantage points where he might hear Miss Elizabeth Bennet when she was speaking with others. It was a method he had used before to discover the true thoughts and nature of a lady of his acquaintance. He had often found their conversations with himself to be contrived and artificial, intended solely to elicit his approbation, and little reflected the speaker's true character; but that by observation of them while they were engaged with others he would come to a more complete understanding of them. Not that he was

Into Hertfordshire

given to prying into the secret affairs of others: only that, while not engaged in conversation himself, he would attend to those around him.

This brought him his first insight into Miss Elizabeth Bennet's character, for she observed his attention and quickly gave him notice of it. He had listened to her while she attempted to persuade Colonel Forster of the --shire Militia, which was then quartered in Meryton, to hold a ball for his officers and the families of the neighbourhood. Her own wit was rather quicker than that of the Colonel, and Darcy smiled once or twice when she managed to outflank his more slowly moving thoughts; she was considerate enough, however, to release him from the trap into which she had put him without ever letting him know he was caught. Caroline Bingley, Darcy observed to himself, would not have been so generous; she would have enjoyed her victory too much to let it go unacknowledged.

She had then turned away from Colonel Forster to speak to her intimate friend, Miss Charlotte Lucas, Sir William's eldest daughter. Darcy had already discovered that the conversation of these two was of particular use in revealing her thoughts and opinions. He therefore moved in the direction they were standing, only to be thus addressed by the lady as he drew near: "Did not you think, Mr. Darcy, that I expressed myself uncommonly well just now, when I was teazing Colonel Forster to give us a ball at Meryton?"

There was a hint of challenge in her tone but her smile was completely charming, and Darcy was pleased by her notice. He stopt politely and responded in a manner that he hoped would draw her into further exchange: "With great energy," he replied, and, matching the tone of her challenge with his own, he added, "but it is a subject which always makes a lady energetic."

"You are severe on us." She met his eye with an arched brow and drew breath to speak further, but her thoughts remained unsaid. "It will be *her* turn soon to be teazed," Miss Lucas intervened quickly, for she sensed a contentious spirit in her friend and did not wish her to dispute with a

Chapter V

man of Mr. Darcy's standing. "I am going to open the instrument, Eliza, and you know what follows."

"You are a very strange creature by way of a friend!" Miss Elizabeth Bennet cried. "Always wanting me to play and sing before any body and every body! If my vanity had taken a musical turn, you would have been invaluable; but as it is, I would really rather not sit down before those who must be in the habit of hearing the very best performers." Darcy was captivated and delighted by her half-jesting, half-serious manner as she protested to her friend, as well as by her well-mannered diffidence towards her own performance.

"But, Lizzy — please? Every one *so* loves to hear you play," Miss Lucas said persuasively. Turning to Darcy she said, "Miss Elizabeth Bennet is a capital performer, for all she protests. I am sure you would rather listen to her play than to discuss the merits of a ball."

Darcy certainly was not inclined to argue that point, and looked at Miss Elizabeth Bennet with polite expectation. The lady relented. "Very well; if it must be so, it must," said she. Assuming an air of resignation and turning to Mr. Darcy, she told him: "There is a fine old saying, which every body here is of course familiar with: 'Keep your breath to cool your porridge'; and I shall keep mine to swell my song."

Her playing was unaffected and pleasing, her voice warm and true, though perhaps the partiality of her friend had somewhat overstated her abilities. But still, Darcy was well pleased to listen to her and even better pleased to have the opportunity to observe her attentively without discourtesy. The face and figure that he had slighted on first sight were now become the only things he could see in a crowded room. And as of this evening he knew her pet name: Lizzy. He liked it: quick and darting on the tongue, it suited her; but he liked her full Christian name better still.

He also reflected with pleasure on the manner in which she had begun their first real exchange: she had fairly accosted him for having listened in on her conversation

Into Hertfordshire

with Colonel Forster. It had been little less than that; yet there was an adorable allure to the manner in which she had confronted him, rather like being attacked by a kitten. No, not a kitten; there was nothing kittenish about Miss Elizabeth Bennet; she had less coquetry about her than any other woman he knew. Darcy was also persuaded that she was possessed of a strong intelligence, which, appearing most often as a display of playful wit, could easily be passed over by the unobservant. He found her conversation enchanting, and began to think what he might do to direct it towards himself. These and other similarly pleasant thoughts occupied him while she continued her song, and, after a gracious protestation in favour of the other ladies present, acquiesced to playing another. After her second piece one of her sisters sat down to play, and all pleasure ended. Where Miss Elizabeth Bennet had made music, even if in a simple style, her sister merely strung notes together; though hers was a more complex piece, her playing had no more spirit than a metronome. Her first selection was plodding and pedantic, and she thereafter gave in to the request of her youngest sister to play dances and reels. This ended all conversation in the room; Darcy could do no more than glare at the Bennet girl playing.

While standing apart and silently castigating the stomping and laughing young people who were dancing, amongst whom he was pained to see his friend Bingley, Darcy was approached by Sir William. That gentleman greeted him with a bow of great deference, and opened a conversation with him by making a pleasant observation on the civilised nature of dance. This did little to soothe Darcy's injured sensibilities: the topic was one he abhorred, and he found Sir William's conversation in general tame and tinged with absurdity, centred as it was around the rights and responsibilities of rank, and his own introduction to that set. Darcy met his conversational sorties with desultory replies until the moment that Miss Elizabeth Bennet happened to walk past them.

Chapter V

"My dear Miss Eliza, why are not you dancing?" cried Sir William, stopping her. "Mr. Darcy, you must allow me to present this young lady to you as a very desirable partner. You cannot refuse to dance, I am sure, when so much beauty is before you."

Darcy suddenly found himself with much more benevolent feelings towards Sir William. What a capital old fellow, he thought. What nice ideas he has—so eager that every one should enjoy themselves. Yet when Sir William took her hand to offer it to Darcy, she withdrew hers with a rapidity that quite surprised Darcy, and hastily said to Sir William with evident sincerity, "Indeed, Sir, I have not the least intention of dancing. I entreat you not to suppose that I moved this way in order to beg for a partner."

Darcy instantly understood: she was too proud to wish to appear as if she were spelling for his attention. Darcy tried to overcome her reticence, saying in his most polished manner, "Miss Elizabeth Bennet, I should be honoured to have your hand for this dance, truly."

Her dignity was unshaken; to Darcy it seemed that she was more determined to resist Sir William's overly-familiar attack and carry her point, than to refrain from dancing, as she said, "I thank you, Sir, but I have no wish to dance this evening."

Sir William persisted: "You excel so much in the dance, Miss Eliza, that it is cruel to deny me the happiness of seeing you; and though this gentleman dislikes the amusement in general, he can have no objection, I am sure, to oblige us for one half-hour."

"Mr. Darcy is all politeness," said she. She favoured Darcy with a faint smile. He was unsure of the meaning of that smile; was she apologising to him for having to turn him down? But there seemed to be an air of mockery in her eyes. Was it for him, or did she have Sir William's well-meaning impertinence in view? Then again, perhaps she thought he was only playing the gallant. Did she think him merely a Society coxcomb, then?

Into Hertfordshire

"He is indeed," Sir William was continuing, "but considering the inducement, my dear Miss Eliza, we cannot wonder at his complaisance—for who would object to such a partner?" At this Miss Bennet only smiled again and arched an eyebrow in Darcy's direction before turning from them with a murmured excuse. She stopped before her friend, Miss Lucas, and began a conversation while still wearing that lovely smile. Then, almost as if she had known he was waiting to see it, her eyes, sparkling with gaiety, travelled back to meet his for a moment before returning to her friend.

Darcy was lifted by this further notice, yet still he wondered at her refusal to dance; he perfectly understood her initial reticence, but why, after he had pressed her, had she continued her refusal? Was she being careful of his tastes, knowing how little he liked to dance? That was certainly possible. Or might it be that she shared his general disdain for the exercise? No, no, she had obviously enjoyed dancing at the assembly. He continued his musings while his eyes followed her, hoping that she might once again reward him with a glance.

"I can guess the subject of your reverie." He turned to see Miss Bingley standing at his shoulder.

Darcy was inwardly amused at the idea of Miss Bingley's reaction to his thoughts, should they be known to her. "I should imagine not," he replied, turning his gaze back in the direction of Elizabeth.

"You are considering how insupportable it would be to pass many evenings in this manner, in such society," she said with that affectation of bored martyrdom so much in vogue among London's fashionable set. "And indeed I am quite of your opinion. I was never more annoyed! The insipidity, and yet the noise—the nothingness, and yet the self-importance of all those people! What would I give to hear your strictures on them!"

"Your conjecture is totally wrong, I assure you." He decided to indulge in a mild bit of wickedness, and actually tell her what he was thinking. "My mind was more agreeably engaged. I have been meditating on the very great pleasure which a pair of fine eyes in the face of a pretty woman can bestow."

Miss Bingley immediately dropt her pretence of boredom and asked with interest which lady might have given rise to such reflections.

"Miss Elizabeth Bennet," he replied, knowing full well that his answer would pique her.

"Miss Elizabeth Bennet!" repeated Miss Bingley. "I am all astonishment. How long has she been such a favourite? —and pray, when am I to wish you joy?"

In spite of her light tone, her eyes held a hard glitter that told Darcy his feint-and-thrust had landed. Careful to conceal his amusement, he replied, "That is exactly the question which I expected you to ask. A lady's imagination is very rapid; it jumps from admiration to love, from love to matrimony, in a moment. I knew you would be wishing me joy."

Taking his teazing answer to indicate that he had not been serious, her eyes softened. Slapping his wrist with her fan she teazed him back at some length, but Darcy paid her little mind; he preferred his own thoughts. He had no opportunity to speak again with Miss Elizabeth Bennet that evening, but his encounter with her had distinctly heightened his interest. He wished for more occasions to associate with her, and rather imagined that Bingley's partiality for the eldest Miss Bennet might be of service in furthering those wishes.

Chapter Six

*D*arcy and Bingley met early the following morning to go shooting, and midmorning found them returning through the fields with three brace of rabbits in their bags. Darcy was pleased, as he was fond of rabbit. The morning had been fine for the season, and the two men took an easy and contented pleasure in their slow ramble back to the Hall. Their conversation ranged widely, and Bingley's new neighbours would scarcely have recognised in his companion the same man who spoke so little in company. Yet, when he was alone with those close to him, whose numbers were exceedingly small, with whom he could put aside the polished forms and formal manners that had been drilled into him while being developed into Darcy of Pemberley, he could allow himself to be at ease.

After a period of aimless conversation, Bingley asked with some seriousness, "Darcy, you have not been yourself of late. Is there anything I can do?"

Darcy looked at his friend with affection. While Bingley's amiability had first drawn his notice, it was his generous nature and true concern for Darcy's well-being that was the foundation of their friendship. With Bingley, as with no other outside his own family, he could count on his friendship and trust his active and disinterested good will. "Thank you Bingley, but no. I am in no difficulties, really. It is only that…well, I suppose I would have to say that the world has weighed rather heavily on me this last year."

"It is not…anything financial, is it? I should be happy to…that is, if you…"

Darcy stopped him. "No, no; my dear Charles, please. The family fortunes are flourishing, I assure you. No, it is just…people — you know: Society, acquaintances, one's associates — the whole blasted breed, or so it seems to me at times. Save for a very small group — yourself included, nat-

Chapter VI

urally — the whole lot of them are no more than a blemish on the face of this, our fair island, and I do believe the place would benefit from a bit of a cleaning."

They walked a little further on in silence, until Bingley said, "For the life of me, Darcy, I cannot imagine what man — or woman, for that matter — could have got across you so." A thought struck him. "It is not Caroline, is it? I know she can be a bit wearing at times, but…"

Darcy waved him off. "No, of course not."

"And Hurst is a bit of a wart, but we could take ourselves off to-night, and forego his company, if you wish."

"Bingley, no!" Darcy smiled and shook his head. "Truly, it has nothing to do with you or yours."

"If it did, would you tell me?" Bingley asked frankly.

Darcy favoured his friend with a grin. "Bingley, I am not a man known for his charitable and forgiving nature. You must face that fact with unflinching fortitude, as have I." Bingley laughed and Darcy went on: "And you know I am not shy with my opinions. Given these unfortunate defects of character, if I did harbour such feelings, would I even be *capable* of dissembling them, supposing that I wished to?"

Bingley gave his friend a wry smile. "Perhaps not."

"No, I should think not," Darcy agreed. "Now, does that put your mind at rest?"

Bingley allowed that it did, but then said, "It still does not explain this mood you have been in. I have never seen you so bleak."

After walking a bit further Darcy seemed to take up a new topic. "Bingley, do you know, I was actually rather pleased for you last summer, when you seemed so taken with Miss Grantley? If we accept that man is meant to marry, then if any one can be happy in the married state, I am sure it will be you. I know none so deserving, nor so likely to succeed. Your informed understanding and great good nature must protect you from most of the unhappiness we see about us."

Into Hertfordshire

Bingley looked at him in surprise; Darcy did not make a habit of speaking his inner thoughts. "It is quite true," Darcy assured him. "But I own that for myself I can entertain no such happy prospects. My expectations are too high and my temper too quick for me to hold out much hope for domestic felicity." They walked on a moment without speaking, as Darcy appeared to be resolving in his mind whether to continue or not. Finally he spoke: "Do you know who set her sights on me last Season? Miss Lavinia Hartsbury."

"No! Darcy, you must be joking! The Rabid Rabbit?" The unfortunate Miss Hartsbury, a remarkably wealthy heiress, even by London standards, was possessed of a very assertive personality and even more assertive front teeth; coupled with a weakness in her eyes that caused her to blink almost incessantly, these prominent qualities of her person were also the source of her soubriquet.

"Unfortunately, my friend, I am in earnest. After nine years in Society without choosing a wife, this attack by Miss Hartsbury forces me to conclude that, inasmuch as I have spurned the attentions of those women in our circle possessing what one would consider the conventional enticements of form, fortune, and standing, those of more marginal charms are becoming emboldened."

"Good Lord!"

"Yes; to such depths I have fallen. I am now become suitable prey for such as Miss Hartsbury."

Bingley laughed with perhaps more open candour than was perfectly polite.

"Well may you laugh," said Darcy dryly. "I fear, however, that I cannot join in your amusement. From my side it was a rather more dour experience, I can tell you. If my reasoning is correct, I shall become the target for every oddity in our acquaintance. And there is worse, still. While I was the object of Miss Hartsbury's campaign I actually asked myself, 'Well, and why not?'"

"Darcy, no!"

Chapter VI

"Bingley, yes. I swear to you on my honour; she is not without character, after all, and I actually asked myself whether it did not follow that, since I obviously had no interest in the women one would consider most eligible, I must be looking for something else. Empirically speaking, the question must be allowed."

"Darcy, one cannot analyse the workings of one's affections like a naturalist studying an insect!"

"No? I beg your pardon; I must have missed that bit at school. Pray, where is that written?"

"The heart and mind are two separate and distinct entities; you cannot examine and control the one by the other," Bingley said with a confident dogmatism which would have better suited a somewhat younger man than himself. "I know you took a First in Philosophy, Darcy, and look upon Socrates as a mere rustic muser, but in one's daily life, with real people, one cannot always resolve the differences between one's emotions and the urgings of reason."

To Darcy this was heresy: his faith in the intellect was complete, and his reliance on his own had always served him well. "Such misguided notions are just what I should expect of man of your sensibilities, Bingley," he scoffed. "How could you possibly know what influence the mind might have on the emotions? You, who have fallen in love at least a dozen times to my certain knowledge, and never subjected your affairs to even the most cursory examination by your higher powers—if we can allow you to possess any." At this Bingley doffed his hat and swatted it at Darcy's head, who dodged sideways with a laugh.

"But come now," Darcy demanded in a provoking manner, "do I understand you then to say that it is not possible to love with both the heart and the mind?"

"No! I am sure that it is possible," stated Bingley with assurance. "It must be! That is my point; such attachments must be possible, else why would they be so much sought after?"

Into Hertfordshire

"Your logic is execrable, but leave that. Allowing your assertion to stand, I must again insist on having your authority for this information; my own experience is to the contrary." When Bingley began to expostulate, Darcy interrupted him: "My own parents excepted, and you know my feelings on that, I cannot claim knowledge of any one so blest. Not only can I point to no one amongst my own acquaintance, never have I even heard of such affection, capable of combining tenderness of regard and honour of the mind. And I am afraid all of literature is against you: I defy you to name one work on the subject, either prose or poetry, wherein the principal characters love well and without conflict—either of reason, honour, or propriety."

"Stories! What do they mean? Of course they're full of drama and anguish; who would want to read about a quiet, happy, faithful love affair? No, we must have conflict to make a tale; but why so in real life?"

"That, I cannot say; but it does most assuredly seem so to me," Darcy said with an air of finality. They were nearly at the Hall. Darcy shook his head like a horse bothered by a fly. "I pray you, Bingley, let us leave off this discussion; I hear it all too often echoing back and forth in my mind: I am heartily tired of it, I can tell you. What say we drop these conies off with Nicholls and get some tea? It has gone a bit chilly."

Chapter Seven

That next Saturday morning Mrs. Hurst and Miss Bingley were to be at home to the ladies of a number of the local families; the two eldest Miss Bennets were to be amongst the company. The attendance of the gentleman was not, strictly speaking, required, but neither of Bingley's sisters were surprised when he arrived in the drawing-room, dressed very smartly indeed, a quarter-hour before the first guests were expected. But that Mr. Darcy should also appear was a source of surprise and comment. Even Bingley took notice, and his thoughts certainly were not centred on Darcy at that moment.

"What! Has the leopard changed its spots?" said he to Darcy. "Have you become a member of Society at last, then? Let me caution you: a man of your advanced years must avoid these sudden shocks to the system, lest you be overset." Bingley, being six years' Darcy's junior, enjoyed reminding him of that fact.

Miss Bingley would not allow this slight to Mr. Darcy to go unchallenged. "Charles, what nonsense! Mr. Darcy knows very well what his duties are as master of Pemberley and our guest; he knows better than you, I dare say, how important it is to observe the conventional civilities in a country society."

Bingley defended himself with feeling, going even so far as to remind his sister of his seniority and of his incontestable right to banter with a friend. When she saw that Darcy was leaning towards her brother's side of the affair, Miss Bingley abandoned her position and demurely accepted his as being proper and correct; as she did so, however, her eye was on Darcy. He noticed her careful observation of his reaction, and interpreted it correctly: she had divined by some means that her occasional lapses of correct behaviour grated on him, and she was assuming this guise of diffidence to curry his favour. His eyes hardened at her calculated dissemblance, but he said nothing.

The argument between the two of them did serve to move the focus of conversation away from him, and that was just as well; the question of what had compelled him to come down was one he could not very well have answered. It certainly was not, he assured himself, that Miss Elizabeth Bennet was expected. With a train of logic worthy of Bingley at his finest, Darcy assured himself that he was safe from any serious interest in her direction, as her connections made any alliance unthinkable, and he was not one to dally with a lady to satisfy his own conceit. And surely, merely to be in her presence was insufficient reason to subject himself to an almost exclusively female society for hours on end. So, while entirely certain of the reasons that did *not* bring him to the drawing-room, he would have been hard pressed to explain the reasons that *did*.

Nevertheless, he did subject himself to such society, and, to those who knew him well, he did so with the appearance of perfect composure—even enjoyment. The only ones in the room, however, who were sufficiently intimate with his ways to be able to observe this were Bingley and his sister Caroline. Bingley's attention, of course, was completely consumed by Miss Bennet; Miss Bingley, on the other hand, was so given over to watching Darcy, that several of her new neighbours wondered at her distraction. Yet there was very little for her to see: he spoke but seldom, and never at length; nor did he appear to have a particular object singled out for discourse. She did observe, though, how often his eyes strayed to Miss Elizabeth Bennet, and how he stilled his own conversation whenever she spoke in his hearing.

Therefore, when, in the course of the following Tuesday morning, Miss Bingley and Mrs. Hurst were discussing how they were to manage to exist another day in the country and Miss Jane Bennet's name was put forward as a means of diversion, Caroline was careful to exclude Miss Elizabeth Bennet from her invitation.

Chapter VII

The invitation to Miss Bennet was a happy one, for it began to rain heavily just before noon and the sisters would be forced to stay indoors all day. The men had taken the coach into Meryton in the late morning, and were to have dinner with the officers under Colonel Forster, so the two sisters would be sorely in need of additional conversational resources.

The men's business in Meryton, being a matter of no less importance than that of procuring Mr. Hurst a new snuff box, was soon over, and they spent a pleasant afternoon watching it rain over tankards of ale in the principal inn of the village. The ale there was not the best to be had in Meryton, but the inn did afford the finest view of the square and therefore the most diverting scenes of people scurrying about their business through the rain. The highlight of the afternoon was the sight of a very rotund and prosperous-looking gentleman, who, descending incautiously from his chaise, sat down heavily in a puddle. The expression on his face was humorous as he sat where he was for several moments without moving, as if unable to believe the position in which he found himself, as was his obvious disgust as he laboriously extricated himself. Mr. Hurst, particularly, was amused by the gentleman's predicament, and laughed heartily when the gentleman lost his balance a second time as he sought to regain his feet.

This episode, with proper embellishment, was retold at the officer's mess with great success. The dinner conversation in general was good, spiced with bits of little-known intelligence on the war with France, caustic wit at the expense of the Government, and the occasional ribald jest. The three gentlemen were feeling very mellow as they returned through the storm to Netherfield.

There, however, they found a mild flurry of activity underway. First off, Bingley received the information that his sisters had invited Miss Bennet to visit in his absence, which he resented as a most invidious stratagem. And secondly, he was informed that she had become ill after her arrival, perhaps as a consequence of having come on horse-

Into Hertfordshire

back through the rain, which made him wild with concern. The apothecary had been sent for, and Miss Bennet had been taken to bed. Bingley ran off to find the apothecary to hear his diagnosis first-hand. It struck Darcy as odd that a country miss should have been so imprudent, as he was himself, after all, Country-bred and thoroughly aware of the probable result of such injudicious behaviour. Had she been a member of London's Society, he would have been tempted to think it had been done intentionally in order to secure a stay at the Hall: a gambit in her bid for Bingley's attentions. But this did not at all fit with what he believed Miss Bennet's character to be; he might readily believe such of Miss Bingley, but Miss Bennet's gentle nature did not seem consistent with the use of arts and cunning in a try for a man's heart.

Once the first fit of activity and concern had subsided, Bingley was, of course, very much the thoughtful host, and nothing was spared for Miss Bennet's comfort. In the morning, as she was no better, Miss Bennet requested that a note be despatched to Longbourn to give her family notice of her illness and to say that she would remain at Netherfield for the time being.

Miss Bennet was too ill to join them at breakfast, but when Darcy was reading the paper over his second cup of coffee, the footman entered to announce "Miss Elizabeth Bennet." Bingley immediately jumped to his feet and cried, "Miss Elizabeth Bennet, I am *so* glad you have come! Your sister, I am sure, will be very relieved to see you."

Darcy, with tolerant amusement at his friend's effusive, if somewhat unpolished, greeting, rose and said with a perfectly correct bow, "Miss Elizabeth Bennet; it is a great pleasure to see you again. I am very sorry that your sister's illness should be the occasion." Her modest curtsey in return pleased him, showing as it did that she shared his appreciation of proper behaviour. Hurst barely sketched a bow from his chair and turned his attention back to his sausages. While Miss Bingley and Mrs. Hurst added their greetings, Darcy took the opportunity to enjoy the picture

Chapter VII

presented by Elizabeth. She had obviously walked the three miles from Longbourn: her face flushed and eyes shining, and with some wind-blown curls having escaped to frame her face like a wild dryad's, she made a portrait worthy of a master's brush. Part of him wished he had been with her; an hour's walk through the Hertfordshire countryside with her would have been charming, indeed. His practical side wondered, though, at her coming: surely Miss Bennet was not *in extremis*; there could be no need for the family to attend her. But the sisters were very close, he knew; therein must lie the reason. He honoured the warm heart that would impel her to make such an effort to comfort a sick sister.

She was shown up stairs directly and Darcy returned to his breakfast. His attention wandered, though, and he laid the paper aside. While the ladies clattered on about the news from London, he could only stare out the window and let his coffee grow cold.

Chapter Eight

*A*fter breakfast Bingley and Darcy had spent half-an-hour in the library, where Darcy had set up to review Netherfield's books and school Bingley in the duties of a landowner. Miss Bingley and Mrs. Hurst went up stairs to entertain and care for the invalid. The apothecary having arrived while the two friends were still at their books, he came to them to announce that Miss Bennet had a severe cold and a fever, and that he had prescribed her some draughts. The palpable obviousness of this pronouncement brought to Darcy's mind one of Voltaire's exercises of wit on physicians: "Doctors pour drugs of which they know little, to cure diseases of which they know less, into human beings of whom they know nothing." Bingley, however, was quite distressed, plying the man with question after question regarding the care and ultimate prognosis of his guest. Darcy was forced to admit to himself that the man handled this inquisition with both good humour and a very appropriate degree of earnest attention. He himself was ready to bite off his friend's head before it was done, and he was not the one having to invent a dozen ways to answer the same question. Mr. Jones assured Bingley repeatedly that Miss Bennet was in no great danger, and he at length released the man. Shortly after the apothecary's departure, the two men took to horse to inspect some outlying barns and fields.

In the afternoon they stood looking at some trenching while Darcy was attempting to explain to Bingley some alterations to the system of ditches that he had employed successfully at Pemberley, but Bingley was not attending. "Bingley, where are your thoughts? You have not heard a word I have said."

"I do apologise, Darcy," his friend answered, contritely. His next comment, though, revealed the subject of his

Chapter VIII

preoccupation: "Do you suppose she is going to be all right?"

Darcy shook his head at his friend. "Good Lord, man, she has a cold, not the pox. Country girls are hardy; she will recover admirably, I assure you."

"But her fever—what if it should worsen? I feel I should be doing something more for her."

This gave Darcy pause. His thoughts flew to Georgiana; he hadn't had a letter from her in a month. "Sometimes the best a man can do is wait," he said quietly. He drew himself up and studied his friend's anxious face. "It *is* getting late," he allowed. "Perhaps we should return?" Bingley agreed in a relieved manner and they rode back to the Hall.

They found, when they arrived, that Miss Elizabeth Bennet was not to return home that evening, for her sister's fever had, in fact, worsened, and Miss Bennet had not wished her sister to leave her. This news heightened Bingley's concerns, and he rushed off to "do something." The news was also of interest to Darcy, although for different reasons, but his attention was quickly turned aside by the arrival of a footman with his post: in it was a letter from his sister.

Pemberley
November 10, —

Dearest Brother,

Please forgive me for not having written before. I know I am not the correspondent I should be, but please do not think me unappreciative of your letters. My spirits have been low and I have lacked the energy to write; but I have read and re-read your last, for the comfort I find in it is my only support. I carry it with me; indeed, at times I cling to it as a drowning man clings to wreckage.

But you must not think me desperate, and thinking of doing myself an injury. No—I see well enough that those are childish, romantic notions,

Into Hertfordshire

and I no longer feel myself a child. I have died once for love—it will not happen again. One who has truly known pain would never seek to inflict it on oneself.

Music is my distraction, and Mrs. Annesley recommends that I ride more; I am trying.

Please, dear Brother, write again soon.
Your sister,
Georgiana Darcy

This short missive created in Darcy an immediate need for a response: this being the first time she had actually written of her feelings, given him an inkling of what she suffered, it was the first opportunity she had given him to assist her in any way. He was greatly relieved that she had at last found the ability to give expression to her emotions; surely this was the first step towards recovery. He sat down immediately to compose his reply, sending Perkins down with his apologies to Bingley.

> Netherfield Park, Herts.
> November 13, —
>
> My dearest Georgiana,
>   I promise I shall write to you every day, now I know you wish for my correspondence…

After two swift paragraphs he paused, uncertain how to go forward: did he offer counsel, did he simply reassure her of his own devotion and tell her to trust to time, or did he adhere to the mundane as a means of diverting her? The answer, he decided, was to do all three. He had always made a point of discussing matters with his sister, not merely issuing directives; she had rewarded his efforts by giving him her confidence, and had always deserved his, by virtue of her good sense. Although her senior by more than ten years, he had always thought of her more as equal than dependant, and had tried to maintain their relationship on that footing; since their parents' deaths they had become

Chapter VIII

very close. As her brother, he felt a deep desire to support her and help her to heal; as the guardian who had failed in his office, he felt it even more his duty to do every thing in his power to assist her. Commanding himself to neither evade the issues nor wander into the merely maudlin, he entered into the most important issue:

> Though I have no experience with a betrayal as deep as the one you have suffered...

After much thought and effort he felt he arrived at the right tone for what was a most difficult piece of writing on the topic of her grief; it had cost him something even to broach the subject at all. But if one wishes to be truthful at all times, then one must be truthful when it is difficult; the greater difficulty was in being truthful without doing harm. At least in writing there was time for reflection, and one might choose one's words carefully. He wished he had his mother's guidance, or some lady on whose good will and good sense he could rely, with whom he might confer on this subject; he wanted help to navigate these waters, for they were dangerous. But that was his burden to bear; he brought his thoughts back to Georgiana, and the reassurances he owed her.

> So, given time, you must heal. Not to the degree that you will ever be exactly the same...

When this part was finished he felt it perhaps a bit excessive, that he had expressed himself too openly; but he could not say less and still say what was in his heart. He would trust to her good will to excuse him for writing so feelingly. The rest was easy.

> Now, let me tell you the news from here...

The final draft took him a great deal of time to complete, and there was just enough time to change before dinner. He entrusted his letter to Perkins to be posted, then went down to the drawing-room.

"Darcy…is all well?" Bingley enquired as he entered.

"Quite well, yes, I thank you," he replied. "A letter from my sister, that is all, and I wished to answer it while it was fresh in my mind."

"'Fresh in your mind'? When would it cease to be 'fresh in your mind'? You have taxed me with minutia from *my* letters a month and more later," his friend berated him with good humour.

"Perhaps that is because *your* follies are more striking than most," Darcy returned. After nearly two hours of sombre effort, he was ready to find pleasure and release in some affable contention with his friend. They continued their banter while they waited on the ladies to appear. The Bingley sisters and Mr. Hurst came down shortly, and Miss Elizabeth Bennet followed soon after; every one moved towards the dining-room on her entrance.

Elizabeth, Darcy noted, wore a gown of a becoming colour, favouring her eyes and her figure, and he could approve her taste in its simple elegance, even though her attire would never pass for fashionable. He spoke his compliments to her and hoped for some part of her attention, but his greeting was mingled with those from the rest of the party and she did not distinguish him in any way. Bingley, of course, wanted to hear immediately how Miss Bennet fared. "Is your sister at all better?" he asked hopefully, before she had even taken her seat. The ladies echoed his concerns and Darcy gave Elizabeth his polite attention, but she had no very favourable reply to offer. She reported that her sister remained in a very feverish condition, and her head ached so badly that she, Elizabeth, had been forced to keep the curtains drawn most of the afternoon to spare her sister's eyes.

"Oh, I know, the poor dear," cried Miss Bingley. "I despise a cold, and to have a headache and a fever as well!"

"Oh, yes!" echoed her sister. "A headache is a most distressing affliction. I cannot abide it, can I, Mr. Hurst?"

Chapter VIII

Hurst glanced up for a moment without comment before returning to his soup. His lady did not seem to mind, or indeed, even to notice, his lack of reply: she went ahead without hesitation: "I become quite a baby. I won't leave my bed until it is gone."

"It grieves me more than I can say that she should have fallen ill after braving that storm on horseback just to be with us," Miss Bingley said. A faint air of contempt for such a low form of transportation suggested itself in her comment.

"Yes, poor dear, she was quite soaked through," put in Mrs. Hurst. Picking up her spoon she concluded, "It is *such* a shocking thing to have a cold."

"Shocking is the very word," agreed Miss Bingley. "An excessively shocking thing, it is." They then dropt the subject and largely ignored Elizabeth, and her sister's health, for the rest of the dinner.

Darcy listened with mild disgust as these repetitious nothings swirled about the table. He wished he could add something of more substance, but he had little opportunity, as Elizabeth was seated on the same side as he, and Miss Bingley was positioned most inconveniently between them. Elizabeth sat facing Hurst, and Darcy knew from experience that he would have little conversation to offer her.

Against the incivility of his sisters, whose regard for Miss Bennet evaporated the moment food touched their lips, Bingley's continued enquiries stood out in marked contrast by their solicitude and obvious sincerity. Indeed, Darcy felt he was having to do too much, and would have taken some of the burden of polite concern off of his friend's shoulders, except that each time he leaned forward to address Miss Elizabeth Bennet, Miss Bingley would lean forward as well with something to ask Mrs. Hurst, who sat across from Darcy. The second time this happened he felt the stirring of suspicion, but when it happened a third time, and even the fourth, he made sure she was acting wilfully to hamper any conversation between Elizabeth and himself. Piqued, he did his best to counteract her ploy, but her

Into Hertfordshire

manœuvre, while simple, was effective at frustrating his attempts. He toyed with the idea of using one of the elaborate coils in her coiffure as a handle to hold her back in her chair so that he might have an unimpeded word with Elizabeth, but he forbore with a sigh, and ceded Miss Bingley her victory.

For her part, Elizabeth did her best to enter into the conversation, but seldom received more than a condescending nod from the sisters in reply. For want of better, she finally addressed Mr. Hurst. That gentleman, who rarely found himself called on to respond to any enquiry, fell back on one of the two topics over which he had any mastery, food and cards, and asked her how she enjoyed the ragout. He, being gourmand rather than gourmet, enjoyed those foods combining strong flavours and heavy texture. Elizabeth answered politely that she generally preferred a plain dish of perfect freshness and natural flavours to the "creations of man's ingenuity." Hurst looked at her as he might have done had she replied that she preferred adders' tongues, and spoke no more to her.

Darcy was determined to speak with her after dinner, but she, perhaps as a result of the incivility she had met with, returned immediately up stairs to her sister. To Darcy's annoyance, Bingley's sisters began their attack on her as soon as her steps were heard upon the stairs.

"Louisa, have you ever seen such manners? She hardly spoke a word, and then only to contradict."

"Indeed, Caroline, her manners are very bad. She combines an entirely baseless pride with impertinent opinions, and scruples not to inflict them on others."

"My very thoughts; and her appearance! What *was* that garment she had on?"

"Oh! Quite," Mrs. Hurst exclaimed, "I believe I saw one like it some ten years ago; but the poor woman who wore it disappeared from all polite society immediately after."

"She has no style, no taste, no beauty…"

Chapter VIII

Her sister interrupted with a superior laugh: "She has nothing, in short, to recommend her, but being an excellent walker. I shall never forget her appearance this morning. She really looked almost wild."

"She did, indeed, Louisa. I could hardly keep my countenance. Very nonsensical to come at all! Why must she be scampering about the country, because her sister has a cold? Her hair, so untidy, so blowsy!" At this Darcy nearly lost *his* countenance; he had retained an altogether different impression of her appearance. He contented himself with directing a whimsical face, compounded of consternation and amazement, at his plate. It passed unnoticed by the two ladies.

"Yes, and her petticoat; I hope you saw her petticoat," said Louisa; "six inches deep in mud, I am absolutely certain; and the gown which had been let down to hide it not doing its office." Here Darcy caught Bingley's eye with a wry expression. Who could think of petticoats when such a singular picture of feminine loveliness was before one?

Bingley gave his agreement to Darcy with a glance and took his sister to task: "Your picture may be very exact, Louisa, but this was all lost upon me. I thought Miss Elizabeth Bennet looked remarkably well when she came into the room this morning. Her dirty petticoat quite escaped my notice."

"*You* observed it, Mr. Darcy, I am sure," said Miss Bingley; "and I am inclined to think that you would not wish to see *your sister* make such an exhibition."

He did not wish to take Miss Bingley's side on any point of this conversation, but he could not but agree with this. The thought of Georgiana wandering across the countryside by herself, at her age, exposing herself to Heaven knows what mischances, made him shake his head with disapprobation. "Certainly not," he agreed shortly.

"To walk three miles, or four miles, or five miles, or whatever it is, above her ankles in dirt, and alone, quite alone! What could she mean by it? It seems to me to show

Into Hertfordshire

an abominable sort of conceited independence, a most Country-Town indifference to decorum."

Bingley lifted his eyes to the heavens and then admonished his sister, "It shows an affection for her sister that is very pleasing."

"I am afraid, Mr. Darcy," Miss Bingley said in an aside to him, "that this adventure has rather affected your admiration of her fine eyes."

This Darcy could easily contradict, and he did so willingly. "Not at all, they were brightened by the exercise."

This reply brought Miss Bingley up short, as Darcy had hoped. Mrs. Hurst took up a new thread: "I have an excessive regard for Jane Bennet, she is really a very sweet girl, and I wish with all my heart she were well settled. But with such a father and mother, and such low connections, I am afraid there is no chance of it."

"I think I have heard you say that their uncle is an attorney in Meryton," Darcy probed gently. He, of course, had had little opportunity to discover anything of the Bennet family, since he could hardly make such enquiries of Miss Elizabeth Bennet herself.

"Yes; and they have another, who lives somewhere near Cheapside," Mrs. Hurst replied.

"That is capital!" her sister exclaimed, and they both laughed behind their hands. It was common for people of their circle to make fun of the name, although there were few who did not have some affairs there; as one of the chief centres of trade in London, most families of standing had interests there, although they generally did not attend to them in person. Darcy was familiar with it, as one of his storage houses was in the vicinity.

Nor did their brother share their amusement. "If they had uncles enough to fill *all* Cheapside," cried he, "it would not make them one jot less agreeable."

At this, Darcy, his thoughts perhaps having a personal application, observed sombrely: "But it must very materially lessen their chance of marrying men of any consideration in the world." It escaped his notice that Bingley's eyes

Chapter VIII

clouded at this, for his own vision was fixed upon some distant point. After this the men had little to add to the conversation, but the ladies, without regard for their friends—either absent or present—continued their entertainment unchecked for some time.

At length the ladies began to rise, as they were going up stairs to visit the patient. While they walked from the room with expressions of concern for their dear friend and hope for her recovery, Darcy reflected on how wonderful it was that the two of them could in one breath be lacerating their friends, and in the next be all that was amiable. After the ladies' departure, Hurst went to his rooms to take his accustomed postprandial nap, which he claimed sharpened his mind for cards later in the evening. Neither Bingley nor Darcy was so desirous of his company as to attempt to dissuade him, so they were left quietly by themselves to dawdle over their wine.

"Darcy, did you mean what you said before, about the Bennet girls being unable to marry well?"

Darcy glanced up at his friend, but Bingley was studying the play of light on the wine as he slowly twisted the stem of his glass. "I am afraid that I did," he replied.

"But why should that be? Surely, in this day and age, two people can marry without all that feudal nonsense about misalliances."

"If by 'this day and age' you are suggesting that we live in such egalitarian times that standing, connections, and fortune no longer matter, I must have missed reading about that revolution in the papers. When did it occur, and how many died on the guillotine?"

Bingley gave an appreciative laugh, but persisted, "Seriously, Darcy—you cannot mean that you, yourself, would not consider offering for a girl unless she was in the first circles."

"'The first circles'? No, surely that is not a requirement. But marry a nobody? Who would countenance her? From what part of society could we form an acquaintance? I have often thought that King Cophetua's beggar maid must have

Into Hertfordshire

had rather a hard time, really. Would you expose the lady of your heart to scorn and disapprobation from your nearest relatives?"

"*My* nearest relatives are my sisters, and they would disapprove of the lady no matter what her rank and fortune; indeed, I cannot think who *would* escape their tongues."

"In that, you are more fortunate than myself. I should have to face down my Uncle Jonathan, the Earl of Andover, although he's a good sort; but my Aunt Catherine—marrying against her wishes would make our current relations with the French seem nothing more than a trifling diplomatic *faux pas*," Darcy said with more seriousness than his words implied.

"Is she as bad as all that, then?" Bingley enquired. "I have heard Colonel Fitzwilliam make some rather amusing comments on her character."

"Lady Catherine de Bourgh is a veritable Gorgon. It is almost incredible to me that she should be related to my mother."

"But she is only your aunt, after all. Why should her wishes weigh so heavily?"

Darcy thought momentarily. "For three reasons, chiefly: firstly, because after my mother's death she became the matriarch of that side of the family; secondly, because her own rank and circumstance is just slightly more important to her than life itself; and thirdly, because she is the most officious creature on Earth, and does not hesitate to thrust her opinions on every one within earshot. The only way I should be able to marry without her consent would be to break off with her completely."

"Lord! Perhaps I am better off without relations!"

Darcy tipped his glass at that in a silent toast. They each withdrew into their own thoughts, and their conversation lagged. Darcy felt the tuggings of that bleak dissatisfaction with life that had plagued him for so many months; reminding himself that he was in company, however, he fought it back down, that he might not give his

Chapter VIII

friend concern. After some minutes they each came back to themselves and the conversation picked up again, passing off onto matters less charged with feeling.

By the time they joined the ladies in the drawing-room, their mood was sufficiently lifted that when Hurst reappeared they were able to meet his challenge to a game of loo with tolerable enthusiasm. The game was tight and the stakes kept improving as time wore on, so that when Miss Elizabeth Bennet joined them late in the evening she was rather intimidated by their play, and chose to read rather than join them at the table. Mr. Hurst expressed amazement that any one might prefer a book to playing cards, but for Darcy it raised her that much higher in his estimation. In his mind reading and understanding were inextricably linked, and the pursuit of understanding was the first measure of the superior person.

To Miss Bingley her arrival was something of a relief, as she had been losing steadily and felt the need of a distraction from the rigors of her pastime. On Elizabeth's refusal to join the game, she said teazingly, "Miss Eliza Bennet despises cards. She is a great reader, and has no pleasure in anything else."

Elizabeth made a polite protest against being given such a character, and declared she took pleasure in a great many things. She drifted over to a table on which were lying a small number of books. "Miss Bennet, may I offer you a greater selection?" Bingley enquired. "You are most welcome to any and all we have in the library here. And I wish my collection were larger for your benefit and my own credit; but I am an idle fellow, and though I have not many, I have more than I ever look into."

"Oh; thank you Mr. Bingley, but I assure you I can do quite well with those already here."

"I am astonished," put in Miss Bingley, who could never allow a conversation to stray too far from her own thoughts and interests, "that my father should have left so small a collection of books. What a delightful library you have at Pemberley, Mr. Darcy." She smiled winningly at him and sought his eyes with hers.

Darcy attempted to deflect both her flattery and her gaze; the former, because he had not contributed even a tenth part of Pemberley's collection, and the latter, as a matter of fixed policy. "It ought to be good," he replied, unfolding and studying his cards resolutely. "It has been the work of many generations."

Miss Bingley, however, brought the compliment back to him, saying, "And then you have added so much to it yourself; you are always buying books."

This gave Darcy some private amusement, as he had often found a visit to the bookseller a convenient means of obtaining relief from Miss Bingley's company in Town. He merely replied, however: "I cannot comprehend the neglect of a family library in such days as these."

"Neglect! I am sure you neglect nothing that can add to the beauties of that noble place." Darcy was certain, in spite of this assurance, that she had in mind one particular addition to his estate that would add immeasurably to its charm in her eyes: a new mistress. She continued, "Charles, when you build *your* house, I wish it may be half as delightful as Pemberley."

"I wish it may," he replied equitably, laying down a winning card with satisfaction. Hurst, who was Darcy's partner, snorted in disgust.

They continued their discussion of Darcy's estate for another hand, until Hurst scolded them all for their inattention. After a moment, though, Miss Bingley started yet another topic designed to demonstrate to Mr. Darcy, and perhaps to others, how deeply interested she was in all his concerns: "Is Miss Darcy much grown since the spring? Will she be as tall as I am?"

"I think she will. She is now about Miss Elizabeth Bennet's height, or rather taller." Darcy, on his side, wished rather to bring the conversation back to their guest, and give her a greater share in it.

Chapter VIII

Miss Bingley began a paean on Georgiana's beauty and accomplishments, but Bingley also attempted to redirect the conversation into a subject of more general interest: "It is amazing to me," said he, "how young ladies can have patience to be so very accomplished as they all are."

"All young ladies accomplished!" exclaimed his sister. "My dear Charles, what do you mean?"

"Yes, all of them, I think. They all paint tables, cover screens, and net purses. I scarcely know any one who cannot do all this, and I am sure I never heard of a young lady spoken of for the first time, without being informed that she was very accomplished."

"Your list of the common extent of accomplishments," said Darcy, pleased to further a topic in which all might have a share, "has too much truth. The word is applied to many a woman who deserves it no otherwise than by netting a purse or covering a screen. But I am very far from agreeing with you in your estimation of ladies in general. I cannot boast of knowing more than half-a-dozen, in the whole range of my acquaintance, that are really accomplished."

"Nor I, I am sure," agreed Miss Bingley. Darcy frowned down on his cards until he could free his countenance of the exasperation he felt. Would she never be still?

"Then you must comprehend a great deal in your idea of an accomplished woman," observed Elizabeth.

Darcy turned quickly to face her. "Yes, I do comprehend a great deal in it," he said with sincerity. But before he could expand on this statement, Miss Bingley interrupted him: "Oh! Certainly," cried she, "no one can be really esteemed accomplished who does not greatly surpass what is usually met with. A woman must have a thorough knowledge of music, singing, drawing, dancing, and the modern languages, to deserve the word; and besides all this, she must possess a certain something in her air and manner of walking, the tone of her voice, her address and expressions, or the word will be but half-deserved."

Into Hertfordshire

All the forms and none of the substance, thought Darcy disparagingly as she spoke. This is exactly the sort of pedestrian and useless course of study followed by every woman in Society: a bit of music, a few amateurish brush strokes, half-a-dozen words of French or Italian, and, of course, every woman's delight: dancing. Add to that the affectation of superior airs, and one arrived at the common, or garden-variety, Society Miss. And, while we are on the subject, what about having manners enough not to be constantly interrupting others?

Not wishing to be discourteous himself, though, he merely said, "All this she must possess," but with a nod towards Elizabeth's book he added, "and to all this she must yet add something more substantial, in the improvement of her mind by extensive reading."

"I am no longer surprised at your knowing *only* six accomplished women," Elizabeth observed. "I rather wonder now at your knowing *any*."

Darcy was delighted to finally have something like a dialogue—how well she expressed herself, and how easily she held her ground against the field! With a smile he said, "Are you so severe upon your own sex as to doubt the possibility of all this?"

"*I* never saw such a woman," she stated firmly. "*I* never saw such capacity, and taste, and application, and elegance, as you describe united." And with this Darcy was forced to agree: when he added his requirements to those of Miss Bingley, he had to allow that his acquaintance failed to supply any such model of womanly excellence. Had he known such a woman, he thought to himself, he would probably have ceased to be single. The remarkable thing was that Elizabeth felt authorised to say so, and, knowing herself to be in the right, did not hesitate to stand against the others.

Mrs. Hurst and Miss Bingley, in spite of their earlier attestations that they knew only a handful who could lay claim to accomplishment, were now quick to claim that many of their friends and acquaintances fit this description,

Chapter VIII

which Darcy knew to be a considerable exaggeration. She and her sister were preparing a concerted attack on Elizabeth when Mr. Hurst, who had been suffering mightily from all this conversation during play, cried foul with such vehemence that all discussion was ended. Darcy was disappointed, for he had felt an interest in the conversation that had been wanting the entire evening. Nor did the conversation ever recover, for Elizabeth left them shortly thereafter to return to her sister.

"Eliza Bennet," said Miss Bingley, when she had quit the room, "is one of those young ladies who seek to recommend themselves to the other sex by undervaluing their own; and with many men, I dare say, it succeeds. But, in my opinion, it is a paltry device, a very mean art."

"Undoubtedly," replied Darcy, seeing the irony of her statement, inasmuch as she was acting in a manner very like the one she was criticising. "There is meanness in *all* the arts which ladies sometimes condescend to employ for captivation. Whatever bears affinity to cunning is despicable." He held her eye long enough for her to colour and turn to her sister to start another idea.

Elizabeth re-joined them only briefly to say that her sister was worse and that she would remain up stairs with her. Bingley was alarmed, and wanted to summon the physician immediately, but Elizabeth requested that any such decision should be delayed until morning. It was so agreed, and she left the company for the night. Darcy retired not much later to his apartments, and fell asleep whilst contrasting Miss Bingley with Miss Elizabeth Bennet in his mind.

Chapter Nine

*M*iss Georgiana Darcy sat at the window of the upstairs salon of Pemberley House, staring disconsolately out across the lawn stretching to the river. Being on the front of the house, the room provided a striking prospect over the park, with the sharp rise of the hills on the other side of the valley, broad brown fields to the left and a stand of tall hardwoods, mostly barren now for the winter, leading away to the right. The muted ochres and browns of the salon walls echoed the colours of the landscape, and her own sombre frame of mind. The river running before the house glinted a leaden grey under heavy clouds, although there had been no rain. She had spent many of her hours seated at this window during the past months, her mood following the falling leaves. The autumnal beauty of Pemberley had held no pleasure for her this year; she could feel nothing, think of nothing, save her pain and mortification.

She came to this place whenever she felt most in need of comfort. In her memory she held many tender and soothing reminiscences of times when her mother had sat with her at that very window when she was a young child, holding her in her lap, her arms around her and her warmth a comfort against her back while they had searched for a glimpse of deer or rabbits, or made pictures in the clouds. Then her mother would make them tea, and they would sit in contented silence, or chatter away an hour, before her mother would go back to her duties about the manor. These memories, indeed, were nearly all that was left to her of her mother, who had died in a riding accident when Georgiana had been but seven years old.

Comfort had been difficult to come by since the prior summer. The man in whom she had believed with utter conviction, whom she had loved with the unquestioning

Chapter IX

certainty of first love, had been exposed as a heartless mercenary who had turned his back on her without a word when her brother had confronted him. Added to this bitterness was the fact that she had consented to an elopement with him, which, in the event of his exposure, left her shamed and repentant before her brother—a brother who had never been other than honest, honourable, and caring and tender of her sensibilities. These pains oppressed her, and at times it felt as though there was some great weight wrapped around her heart, making it hard to breathe, hard to think, and an agony to feel. No sooner would she push back the heartache of her false lover than she would be struck by the horror of what she had almost done to her ancient family's honour and reputation. There seemed nowhere to turn where she might find refuge from her injured feelings.

To-day she was very low, indeed, for she had yet another care to oppress her: she might expect to hear back from her brother to-day. She had written to him nearly a week before, for the first time in a long while, and had asked him for a letter in return. On the day she had written him, her spirits had been at their lowest, and with a daring she wondered to recall, she had written about her pain. She had never dared do so before; her sense of shame always overcame her, even in the face of her brother's kindness and concern. Now, however, she feared that she had said too much, and that her foolishness would anger him. That would be the worst, the most insupportable of all. She had only seen her brother truly angry once in her entire life, when he had arrived to find her lover with her at Ramsgate. His anger against Wickham had been cold and terrible, petrifying in its intensity. To have that anger directed against herself would be, she thought now with dread, the crumbling of her last support. Towards her he had never been anything but gentle and compassionate, even at Ramsgate, but, in her solitude and bitter pain, she could not but fear that now, having expressed herself with too much sensibility for one so cool-headed and rational as her brother, this

Into Hertfordshire

last succour would fail her. One's fears must always multiply during a period of anxious anticipation, and five days could become an eternity to one already wounded in spirit.

A soft knock at the door announced Mrs. Annesley, her companion. Mrs. Annesley was a sensible woman of middle years, recently widowed, who felt the wisdom of allowing Miss Darcy time to herself each day. Her husband had been in charge of the affairs of one of Mr. Darcy's associates in Town, and his untimely death had left her in need of a post just at the time Miss Darcy was in need of a companion. It had suited her to leave London for a time, and so she had accepted Mr. Darcy's offer and travelled directly to Pemberley. Georgiana felt for her recent loss and admired her resolution and strength under an affliction that must be even more devastating than her own. On Mrs. Annesley's side, she found the young lady's gentleness most engaging to her feelings. Knowing only that she had lately suffered a "disappointment", she nonetheless entered into Georgiana's cares with deep concern, and benefitted not a little by having someone to minister to other than herself.

Georgiana turned towards the door. Mrs. Annesley entered, a letter in her hand. "You have a letter from your brother, Miss Darcy, dear," said she.

Georgiana rose from her window seat and reached out a hand which she was careful to keep from trembling. She stood with the letter in her hand, but made no move to open it. Neither spoke for a moment, while Georgiana stood quite still. Mrs. Annesley smiled at her gently, then closed the door behind her as she left the room. Georgiana then looked down at the letter: it was thick, thick enough to hold volumes of censure and disgust; yet the hand of the direction seemed normal. She turned it over, hoping to find some hint of its contents, but her brother's customarily neat habits of execution had left the envelope a blank. There was nought to be seen from the outside—she must open it.

> Netherfield Park, Herts.
> November 13, —

Chapter IX

My dearest Georgiana,

I promise I shall write to you every day, now I know you wish for my correspondence. And do not feel burdened by the need to reply; do so at your convenience, and if you have anything to say.

Dearest, are you sure that I had not better be at home with you? There is nothing here that requires my presence, and even if there were, nothing could take precedence over your slightest needs. Tell me instantly if you want me, and I shall be home before the sun rises twice.

Though I have no experience with a betrayal as deep as the one you have suffered, I do know that even the deepest wounds must heal in time, if we can but survive the initial blow. This you have done, and what is more, you have *felt* this to be true, which is infinitely more important than being *told*, no matter by whom. I refer to your realization that harming yourself is not a solution. Pain so great as to overwhelm the mind and body can, most assuredly, result from such injuries as yours. *Felo de se*, in these cases, is no more than a delayed reaction to the original attack; that you do not feel such an exigence is proof that you have not taken mortal injury. This is why I can confidently say that you will heal. You may not have had these thoughts in mind when you wrote me those lines, but, perhaps, now that I have presented them in this light you might see them as I do. And you ought to know that I was never alarmed by any thought of your doing yourself an injury; I knew you would never have done anything rash, for I know you. Whether you made a deliberate decision, or were simply acting according to your nature, I was certain that you could never conduct yourself in a way that would harm others, as such an act must invariably do.

Into Hertfordshire

So, given time, you must heal. Not to the degree that you will ever be exactly the same as you were before, I know, and that saddens me immeasurably; but neither will you be crippled by the scars — that I swear. It was I who failed to protect you, and it is upon me to see to your recovery. If the path to restoring your strength leads us to the ends of the earth, if I must ransom our lands and impoverish every one of our connections, I will see you whole again. Please, Dearest, please do not hold back if there is anything you want, anything you desire, anything that holds even the faintest hope of cheering you.

Now, let me tell you the news from here. Mr. Bingley has, seemingly, managed yet again to stumble into a pleasant situation; his propensity for leaping blindly is surpassed only by his great good fortune in not cracking his noggin on landing. With no more than half-an-hour's investigation, he has managed to secure a lovely estate. Of course, Hertfordshire is not Derbyshire, but still and all it is handsome and well-suited to his needs. Miss Bingley and Mr. and Mrs. Hurst are here with us, so Miss Bingley has a willing audience for her wit and there is no want of loo and whist. Mr. Bingley is smitten again, this time with a country miss of little standing and no connections, but a lovely girl nonetheless, whose smiles are the only ones I have ever seen that outshine Bingley's own. She also is here, owing to having been taken ill during a visit to Miss Bingley. She is attended by one of her sisters, whose conversation and countenance have been among the brighter notes of this expedition into the country. But now, Dearest, I must leave off to post this and go down to dinner. I promise to write more fully to-morrow. Until then, know that you are in my heart and thoughts.

Chapter IX

Your devoted, albeit distant, brother,
Fitzwilliam Darcy

Georgiana's fears, which had so consumed her, were now fled; they were but smoke and mist, cleared from her vision by her brother's steadiness. Her relief was great, but her sense of obligation and gratitude greater still. A second reading gave her much to think about; her immediate relief past, she was able to attend more carefully to the letter's contents, and her feelings were scarcely less moved by the force of his arguments than by his gentleness and sincerity in placing them before her.

Georgiana was an intelligent and thoughtful young woman; but where her brother's intellect and understanding were fixed on the world around him, hers were directed inward. Indeed, she was so careful an observer of her own actions and motivations, as to have convinced herself of many flaws that no one else could have detected. It was, in large part, this tendency towards self-criticism that had made these last months so difficult for her, as it had amplified her guilt and remorse to a degree unusual in one so young. This same tendency also caused her to be diffident with others; shy from a conviction of her flaws, rather than from a natural disinclination to company. Her father's oft-repeated admonition to "stand tall, my dear, like a Darcy," had failed in one respect: while she had, indeed, a very erect bearing, she had not imbibed that pride of self that had been her father's true desire. But her reserve in company, coupled with her position, her upright and elegant figure, and her clear, intelligent gaze, had combined to give her an unwarranted reputation for pride eclipsed only by her brother's.

Her thoughtfulness now demanded an early answer to her brother's letter. With a promise to herself to keep her sensibilities in check, she began.

Pemberley
November 15, —

Into Hertfordshire

Dearest Fitzwilliam,

Forgive me, please, for not having written this last week, but in truth I feared to do so until I received your reply. I so dreaded your censure; you may imagine my relief, therefore, when…(she struck through this last, and began again). Words cannot say how much it means to me to have your strength to support me. Thank you again and again for the kindness and gentleness of your instruction; you are the most compassionate and generous brother any one might wish for.

What you have written reasons strongly with my thoughts, and while I am not as accustomed to using logic to guide my life as you are, of course, I own that your arguments appear to me to hold a great deal of truth. Never before had I felt the full force of life's sorrows—not even when Mother and Father passed—but even so I knew I should survive the events of July. Even when I could not see how or why I should live, I knew that I should not succumb to my pain. Until now I had seen this as a punishment; I could not see, as you did, what it must say about eventual recovery.

But while your reassurances are felt more deeply, perhaps, than you can know, in a way it is almost more important to me to know that some one like yourself can possess such acute sensibilities; if not for you and the dear Colonel, I must sometimes despair of there being any feeling among your sex at all. It is hard for me to believe that you and the man who betrayed me are of the same race! How one could be so cruel, yet seem so sweet, and the other be so warm and sensible, yet seem so cool-headed, is beyond my understanding. How will I ever know how to trust, if such a one as he can disguise his true nature so completely? Do we ever learn to distinguish? But no;

Chapter IX

did not he deceive Father? Oh, Fitzwilliam, tell me how I shall ever trust again!

No; I must not let my distress distort my thoughts—pray forgive my lapse. My doubts press upon me too strongly at times, but it passes. There *is* truth and warmth among my fellow creatures—in my family there is, I know: you, the Colonel, dear Aunt Eleanor and Uncle Jonathan, these are my proofs. I must hold firmly to these, and barricade my heart against the rest. My family shall be my bastion and my talisman. There, it shall be so. Yes; I have my anchor, and I shall no longer be tossed about in the storm. I shall learn to be myself again, I promise you, dear Brother.

Your idea of impoverishing the family I found inexpressibly shocking, Fitzwilliam; I am mortified by the very notion. I should not have thought it possible that you might be so sensible of my condition as to even imagine such a thing. I could never allow you to take any step that might injure our family further on my behalf. You must never think on this subject again. I am very aware of the trouble I have been, and I am ashamed to have caused you such difficulty and distress; I know it must have cost you a great deal to write on such distasteful matters without giving way to a very natural abhorrence. Your clear-headedness amazes me; I am not yet able to keep my despair from intruding into my calmer thoughts, although I am trying with each day to push it farther from me. Your composure in dealing with these matters will be my model, and I shall try with every day to gain a better mastery over myself.

Do not concern yourself by your absence; I need reflection more than diversion. Do not, therefore, leave your friends on my account. Know, too, that I would not hesitate to call you home if there were need; but though there are times, I confess, that I would be glad of the sight of you (never more than at this moment, dear Brother), I still feel as I did before: that it is best that I have this time to myself.

Tell me more of Mr. Bingley's 'country miss,' and her sister—I have never heard you speak so of a lady; she must be beyond amiable to have earned your approbation. You approve of her conversation and countenance, but what is she like? Is she kind? She is there to care for her sister, so I assume she must be good-hearted. What are her accomplishments? What is it about her that has won your good opinion? You must write more fully.

In closing let me thank you again, Brother dear, not so much for your letter as for being yourself. I feel most fortunate, yet so undeserving, to have your love and care.

Yours, most truly,
Georgiana Darcy

That the reassurances of those we love are efficacious in overcoming adversity is well known, and their effects are nowhere seen as clearly as in the untroubled sleep of an unburdened soul. Georgiana slept well that night, for the first time in many weeks.

Chapter Ten

Mornings at Netherfield Hall were quiet, with that soft and serene quiet found only in the country. Darcy enjoyed the early hours of the day, before the rest of the household was stirring; savouring the calm, taking his first cup of tea or coffee in the empty breakfast salon, and watching the morning unfold. There was the paper to read, correspondence to attend to, or even just one's own thoughts to engage one's mind while the faint stirrings of birds and wind from out of doors blended soothingly with the muted comings and goings of the servants. And, agreeably, his friend would usually appear downstairs just at the time when he had finished sorting through his thoughts and began to think of occupation.

That morning when Bingley came down he was in better spirits than he had been since Miss Bennet had been taken ill; he informed Darcy that she was showing signs of improvement, but that "poor Miss Elizabeth Bennet" had spent almost the entire night by her sister's side. Darcy, whose father's death had left his own sister in his care when she was but eleven years of age, thought of times he himself had sat up with her when she was ill, and all his sympathies were with Elizabeth.

But he heard with consternation that, in spite of Miss Bennet's amendment, Mrs. Bennet's presence had been requested, for Elizabeth apparently wished her mother's judgement on her sister's health. On hearing this, and fearing all the discordant noise she would bring with her to shatter the tranquillity of the morning, Darcy immediately proposed to take himself out for a ride, until this matriarchal visit should have ended. But Bingley beseeched Darcy so earnestly not to abandon him, that Darcy allowed himself to be persuaded.

Into Hertfordshire

Mrs. Bennet arrived with her two youngest daughters very shortly after breakfast. A brief calculation convinced Darcy that they must have been uncommonly quick in responding to the note that had been sent, and he deduced that they were as eager to be at Netherfield as they were to see the invalid. They were taken up stairs directly to see Miss Bennet. After some time, Miss Bingley brought them down to the breakfast parlour, accompanied by Elizabeth, whereupon Mrs. Bennet made three things clear: she was quite content to forego the pleasure of her daughters' company at home yet a while; she wished the family to know that she was profusely grateful for their hospitality; and she highly approved of the furnishings, views, and general splendour of Netherfield. Her conversation was dizzying in its inconsistency: flitting from topic to topic, she never staid with one long enough to say anything of consequence. She would start a dozen ideas in half that many sentences, without so much as a pause for breath in between.

Speaking of the care her daughter had received, she expressed herself thus: "I am sure, if it was not for such good friends I do not know what would become of her, for she is very ill indeed, and suffers a vast deal, though with the greatest patience in the world, which is always the way with her, for she has, without exception, the sweetest temper I ever met with. I often tell my other girls they are nothing to *her*. You have a sweet room here, Mr. Bingley, and a charming prospect over the gravel walk. I do not know a place in the country that is equal to Netherfield. You will not think of quitting it in a hurry, I hope, though you have but a short lease."

Darcy shook his head slightly, trying to conceive what sort of mental processes could give rise to such a verbal tangle. Her thoughts called to mind a moth fluttering around a candle; circling it up, down, and sideways, but never reaching the objective it strove for. Mrs. Bennet's principal object, however, was clear enough; she wished to promote Bingley's attentions to Miss Bennet, and his gen-

Chapter X

eral contentment with the neighbourhood, by any and every means in her power.

Bingley, picking up only the very last subject of her torrent, replied: "Whatever I do is done in a hurry, and therefore if I should resolve to quit Netherfield, I should probably be off in five minutes. At present, however, I consider myself as quite fixed here."

"That is exactly what I should have supposed of you," said Elizabeth teazingly. Darcy thought she looked quite well this morning, in spite of her long night, and admired her for having the energy even to appear in company, let alone contribute to it by exerting her social powers.

Bingley and Elizabeth amused themselves in a light badinage on how open was Bingley's character, and how easy to comprehend, until her mother broke in scoldingly: "Lizzy, remember where you are, and do not run on in the wild manner that you are suffered to do at home." Elizabeth's eyes took on a pained expression: to be reprimanded in such a public manner for holding such an innocuous and amiable conversation! Darcy could not tell whether she was more ashamed of having received the rebuke, or of her mother for having uttered it.

"I did not know before," Bingley put in quickly, trying to pass over the mother's interruption, "that you were a studier of character. It must be an amusing study."

Elizabeth brightened again and replied, "Yes, but intricate characters are the *most* amusing. They have at least that advantage."

Darcy knew from experience that, while the country had its charms, the number of subjects available for such study was very limited. He had himself been struck forcibly by that realisation when he entered University: the range of ideas and characters he had encountered there had been a revelation. He had suspected early on in their acquaintance that Miss Elizabeth Bennet had not spent her entire life in Hertfordshire, as thoroughly as her understanding was developed; perhaps she might offer a clue if the current topic were continued. He said, "The country can in general supply but a few subjects for such a study. In a country neighbourhood you move in a very confined and unvarying society."

"But people themselves alter so much," Elizabeth replied reasonably, "that there is something new to be observed in them forever."

Her reply did not give Darcy the information on her history he sought, but he was on the verge of agreeing to her point when Mrs. Bennet rushed in with: "Yes, indeed. I assure you there is quite as much of *that* going on in the country as in Town."

There was a moment's silence as a general embarrassment prevented comment. On his side, Darcy was not certain he even understood to what she might be referring with this assurance, but her manner was clear enough: she was attempting to affront him, and doing so with a degree of malice he found quite unaccountable.

Insensible of the company's common discomfort, Mrs. Bennet sailed on: "I cannot see that London has any great advantage over the country, for my part, except the shops and public places. The country is a vast deal pleasanter, is not it, Mr. Bingley?"

"When I am in the country," replied he with equanimity, "I never wish to leave it; and when I am in Town it is pretty much the same. They have each their advantages, and I can be equally happy in either."

"Aye—that is because you have the right disposition. But that gentleman," she indicated Darcy with a curt nod, "seemed to think the country was nothing at all."

"Indeed, mamma, you are mistaken," cried Elizabeth in an earnest attempt to erase, or even simply to ease, the open censure under which Darcy suffered. "You quite mistook Mr. Darcy. He only meant that there was not such a variety of people to be met with in the country as in Town, which you must acknowledge to be true." Darcy was gratified by Elizabeth's defence of him, even though it was scarcely necessary; his disdain for her mother left him indifferent to her attack.

Chapter X

Mrs. Bennet continued: "Certainly, my dear, nobody said there were; but as to not meeting with many people in this neighbourhood, I believe there are few neighbourhoods larger. I know we dine with four-and-twenty families."

The absurdity of this statement gave the Bingley sisters some little amusement, and Bingley himself could do no better than stare fixedly ahead; even *his* powers of affability were overcome. In London there might be thrice that many couples at a simple dinner party. Darcy, too, was shocked at such an amalgamation of ignorance and conceit, and had she been other than she was, he might have had something to say in response to her; but as it was, to speak one's disapprobation would be rather like starting an argument with a barking dog: merely an annoyance to both parties. He therefore schooled his temper and held his tongue. This was a skill in which his father had tutored him: allowing those of lesser abilities or positions to speak, without feeling the need to contend with them—although he had seldom before been so challenged in the exercise of that skill.

Elizabeth, in hopes of turning aside her mother's thoughts, asked if her friend Miss Lucas had been to visit in her absence. "Yes, she called yesterday with her father," replied her mother. "What an agreeable man Sir William is, Mr. Bingley—is not he? So much the man of fashion!" This comment sent the Bingley ladies into a perfect spasm of suppressed laughter. "So genteel and so easy! He has always something to say to everybody. *That* is my idea of good breeding; and those persons who fancy themselves very important, and never open their mouths, quite mistake the matter." This was spoken quite pointedly at Darcy, and Miss Bingley stared wide-eyed, first at her, then at Mr. Darcy.

Good Lord! thought Darcy. *Your* idea of good breeding, Madam? What could you know of good breeding? He turned away to the window. If one learnt nothing else at Oxford, the art of the cut was practised most assiduously by all students. Darcy knew from long experience that a cool, uncaring dismissal was the most effective answer to spleen;

Into Hertfordshire

to argue was to lend unwanted significance to the other person.

"Did Charlotte dine with you?" Elizabeth asked then, trying desperately to keep her mother on a neutral topic.

"No, she would go home. I fancy she was wanted about the mince-pies. For my part, Mr. Bingley, *I* always keep servants that can do their own work; my daughters are brought up differently. But everybody is to judge for themselves, and the Lucases are a very good sort of girls, I assure you. It is a pity they are not handsome! Not that *I* think Charlotte so *very* plain—but then she is our particular friend."

"She seems a very pleasant young woman," said Bingley.

"Oh! dear, yes; but you must own she is very plain." Darcy shook his head as he stared out across the park. There it was again, that willingness in a woman to malign her nearest acquaintance; even as the thought crossed his mind, however, it occurred to him that he had never heard Elizabeth do so. Mrs. Bennet went on: "Lady Lucas herself has often said so, and envied me Jane's beauty. I do not like to boast of my own child, but to be sure, Jane—one does not often see any body better looking. It is what every body says. I do not trust my own partiality. When she was only fifteen, there was a gentleman at my brother Gardiner's in Town so much in love with her that my sister-in-law was sure he would make her an offer before we came away. But, however, he did not. Perhaps he thought her too young. However, he wrote some verses on her, and very pretty they were."

"And so ended his affection," Elizabeth intervened in a determined manner. Darcy pitied her the necessity of having constantly to create diversions to deflect the conversation around her mother's want of sense. "There has been many a one, I fancy, overcome in the same way. I wonder who first discovered the efficacy of poetry in driving away love!"

Chapter X

Darcy drew away from the windows, attracted by the return of rational speech, especially from that quarter. "I have been used to consider poetry as the *food* of love," said he, pleased by both an intelligent subject and the opportunity to take control of the conversation away from Mrs. Bennet. Elizabeth's ability to take up a position that was the direct opposite of conventional wisdom and make it seem reasonable was one of the first indications he had had of her intellect; her playful displays of wit always amused and captivated him. But, still—such a mother! How a woman with so little sense, humour, and understanding could have given birth to a daughter possessed of so much of each, seemed almost to defy the laws of nature.

"Of a fine, stout, healthy love it may," Elizabeth replied to his sally, her manner more relaxed now that the topic was launched and her mother's voice was stilled. "Every thing nourishes what is strong already. But if it be only a slight, thin sort of inclination, I am convinced that one good sonnet will starve it entirely away."

To this Darcy could think of no adequate reply, but he smiled pleasantly at her, to acknowledge her wit. He wondered again where she had been educated; it must have been in Town, yet her air was nothing like that of a London Miss. They both were casting about for another topic when her mother again took up the reins of the conversation. The company held its collective breath, but at least on this occasion she did not direct her comments at Darcy; she satisfied herself with additional expressions of gratitude to Bingley, which, once accepted, left nothing for her to do but order her carriage.

Elizabeth returned to her sister's side, and Bingley's sisters began to amuse themselves by retailing the conversations of the last hour to one another. As they carried on, Darcy recalled a time when Miss Bingley had come down to breakfast after a poor night's sleep: she had behaved like an ill-tempered child. He wondered how she might have managed this morning, had she been in Elizabeth's place. How she must suffer under her mother's influence! Not only that,

Into Hertfordshire

but he could see clearly what little chance she had of meeting and marrying a man capable of recognising and cultivating her depths. He envisioned a sad future laid out before her: marriage to some countrified gentleman of little means and less intellect, the slow wasting away of her vivacity and wit, the grinding effects of keeping a household and raising children on an inadequate income; and all this because of a mother whose obvious deficiencies would force any one with decent connections to conclude that such objectionable traits could not be allowed into one's own family. If she could but be persuaded even to hold her tongue, her daughters would be infinitely better off. He felt for Miss Bennet's situation, and pitied her from his heart.

Chapter Eleven

The remainder of the morning passed rather slowly. Darcy and Bingley forgave each other a mutual truancy in their study of the Netherfield books, and the ladies spent much of the day up stairs to aid with Miss Bennet's convalescence. Later, after several long and largely silent hours within doors, the gentlemen decided to see if there was any sport to be had, and so took all the dogs and most of the fowling pieces out for a tramp. The most they got out of it was exercise and reddened cheeks, for the day was raw and windy, and game was scarce. Darcy was glad of a hot bath when they returned, and spent the time until dinner in front of a fine blazing fire, while he attended to a letter from his steward at Pemberley.

After dinner, when the men joined the ladies in the drawing-room, Darcy settled himself in to write to Georgiana as he had promised he would. Bingley was challenged by Hurst to piquet, whose lady sat with him for luck. Miss Bingley devoted herself, as best she could, to supporting Darcy in writing his letter. Elizabeth appeared somewhat later, reporting that her sister was resting well and continued to improve. She then took up some needlework and quietly attended to their conversation.

Miss Bingley's efforts on Mr. Darcy's behalf consisted of a constant barrage of questions and commendations, forcing Darcy to call on every ounce of his civility to prevent her interruptions from causing him to respond with a breach of manners. But he was satisfied on one point: he was able, by means of his collected and indifferent answers to Miss Bingley, to demonstrate to Elizabeth how little Miss Bingley's attentions meant to him. His motives for so doing were not something to which he truly gave much reflection, but he did derive a decided satisfaction from letting Eliza-

Into Hertfordshire

beth see his general apathy towards Miss Bingley's approbation.

His progress through his letter ran thus:

> Netherfield Hall
> November 14, —
>
> Dearest Georgiana,
> I hope you have had time to read and reflect on my letter of yesterday; as I think back on it I can find no part of it that I would amend. I trust you will forgive me for writing so openly and feelingly on such subjects, knowing as you do that I should never write so to another. But with you I have no reservations, nor do I fear that I might be misunderstood, as you will always honour me with the benefit of your trust and your good heart. But as I have no desire to lecture on these topics, I shall henceforth hold my thoughts on the subject in abeyance, until you have had an opportunity to reply.
>
> Miss Bingley here asks that I convey to you her compliments, and her delight in the prospect of seeing you at Christmas. We are in the drawing-room after dinner; she sits near me as I write, and sanctions my efforts with her fullest approval and encouragement. If, therefore, my letter seems stilted or haphazard in its construction, or some tinge of exasperation creeps into it, I pray you will forgive me and attribute it to the appropriate cause.
>
> While here at Netherfield I have encountered rare new levels of both sense and nonsense; here I have met with one whose nonsensical views and mental dishevelment surpasses any other in my experience. This is one Mrs. Bennet, who is mother to the two young ladies I told you of yesterday. She is a veritable caricature of unreason, unable to

Chapter XI

hold onto a single thought long enough to complete an intelligible sentence, and yet at the same time maintaining a complete assurance of the sagacity of her judgement and the rectitude of her opinions. I have been in her company now several times, and never once has she offered a comment worth the hearing. Her two eldest daughters, I am happy to say, the ones who are staying presently at Netherfield Hall, have escaped the misfortune of sharing their mother's affliction. She has three other daughters, however, who are certainly infected with the disorder, although not to such an acute degree.

Notwithstanding, the second Miss Bennet, Miss Elizabeth Bennet, is that very one whose sense and understanding is so superior to any other lady's in my acquaintance. She has just joined us in the drawing-room after tending to her sister throughout the day, and most of the night prior. Save for you, she shows the greatest good sense and warmest regard for others I have ever seen combined in any of my fellow creatures.

At this point Miss Bingley ventured the observation that Miss Darcy would be delighted to receive such a letter. Darcy vouchsafed no reply.

"You write uncommonly fast," said she, persisting in her attempts to draw his attentions to herself.

Unable to avoid her conversational sorties entirely, he replied as briefly as he might: "You are mistaken. I write rather slowly."

"How many letters you must have occasion to write in the course of a year! Letters of business, too! How odious I should think them!"

"It is fortunate, then, that they fall to my lot instead of to yours."

"Pray tell your sister that I long to see her."

"I have already told her so once, by your desire."

Into Hertfordshire

"I am afraid you do not like your pen. Let me mend it for you. I mend pens remarkably well."

"Thank you—but I always mend my own."

This ended Miss Bingley's contributions for a time. Miss Elizabeth Bennet, he observed, had something of a smirk hovering about her lips; he was pleased by this evidence of her notice—and she obviously saw how hopeless were Miss Bingley's attempts to secure his favour. He continued with good heart:

> Between Miss Elizabeth Bennet and Miss Bingley there exists a great disparity of personality, and I have been afforded no small measure of entertainment by studying the difference between Country manners and Town manners. Miss Bingley is every inch the Society Miss, as you know, having lived almost exclusively in London, whereas Miss Elizabeth Bennet's manners have nothing fashionable about them—she, as I believe, having been brought up largely here in Hertfordshire. It is interesting to contrast her character and Miss Bingley's: she is sincere where Miss Bingley is witty, witty where Miss Bingley is affected, charming where Miss Bingley is smart, warm where Miss Bingley is well-mannered. And Miss Elizabeth Bennet is possessed of a singular intellect: I have seen her run verbal circles around a staunch military man, yet show such rare concern and compassion as to do so without giving him so much as a hint of what she was about, and taking no advantage of the poor man at all. Upon your brother she has turned her wit like unto a well-honed rapier, and yet has done so in the most charming manner imaginable. She is very amiable, and adores dancing (although, to say the truth, she has turned down my hand), and even though the society hereabouts offers little by comparison with her own talents, she remains

Chapter XI

thoroughly modest, unaffected by the awareness she could scarcely avoid of her own superior gifts.

I must digress again, as Miss Bingley, having earlier commended the speed and evenness of my writing, now wishes me to convey to you her "raptures" over the design for a table you made last summer, to express how delighted she is to hear of your improvement in music (forgive me; I must confess that I often boast about you), and diverse other expressions of esteem. In truth, Dearest, I am not certain whether all this is meant for you, or even me; I suspect that it may have to do with Miss Bingley's quest for ascendancy over Miss Elizabeth Bennet. Her expressions of approbation may be nothing more than a means of display; making mention of such things as an indication of the superior society in which she travels, and to which Miss Elizabeth Bennet could have no access at all.

All this gives me to feel how fortunate you and I have been to be raised in Derbyshire, and yet to have had frequent access to Town; for the Country holds England's heart, while London is the seat of its intellect and initiative. We therefore have the best of both worlds: the heart to know what is good and right, and the head to seek and to savour it.

Miss Bingley interrupted Darcy yet again, this time to praise the length of Darcy's letter and to assert that any one capable of writing such long letters with ease could not write ill. Her brother, who could no longer sit through her excessive exhibition of regard and approval in silence, broke in with: "That will not do for a compliment to Darcy, Caroline, because he does *not* write with ease. He studies too much for words of four syllables. —Do not you, Darcy?"

Into Hertfordshire

"My style of writing is very different from yours," replied he. He stole a cautious look at Elizabeth to observe her reaction to Bingley's attack on him; it was unkind of Bingley to accuse him thus in company—surely he never did as much to Bingley in her sister's presence! Elizabeth did raise her eyes from her needlework, but nothing other than amused interest showed in them.

"Oh!" cried Miss Bingley, "Charles writes in the most careless way imaginable. He leaves out half his words, and blots the rest."

"My ideas flow so rapidly that I have not time to express them," said Bingley lightly, "by which means my letters sometimes convey no ideas at all to my correspondents."

"Your humility, Mr. Bingley," said Elizabeth, taking his side against his sister's disparagement, "must disarm reproof."

"Nothing is more deceitful," Darcy struck back at Bingley, cocking an eyebrow in his direction, "than the appearance of humility. It is often only carelessness of opinion, and sometimes an indirect boast."

Bingley, while knowing he stood little chance of besting his friend in such discourse as this, nonetheless countered with: "And which of the two do you call *my* little recent piece of modesty?"

"The indirect boast—for you are really proud of your defects in writing, because you consider them as proceeding from a rapidity of thought and carelessness of execution, which if not estimable, you think at least highly interesting. The power of doing anything with quickness is always much prized by the possessor, and often without any attention to the imperfection of the performance. When you told Mrs. Bennet this morning that if you ever resolved on quitting Netherfield you should be gone in five minutes, you meant it to be a sort of panegyric, of compliment to yourself—and yet what is there so very laudable in a precipitance which must leave very necessary business un-

Chapter XI

done, and can be of no real advantage to yourself or any one else?"

"Nay," Bingley protested, "this is too much, to remember at night all the foolish things that were said in the morning. And yet, upon my honour, I believed what I said of myself to be true, and I believe it at this moment. At least, therefore, I did not assume the character of needless precipitance merely to show off before the ladies."

"I dare say you believed it," allowed Darcy. "But I am by no means convinced that you would be gone with such celerity. Your conduct would be quite as dependant on chance as that of any man I know; and if, as you were mounting your horse, a friend were to say, 'Bingley, you had better stay till next week,' you would probably do it, you would probably not go—and, at another word, might stay a month."

"You have only proved by this," Elizabeth said, again coming to Bingley's defence, "that Mr. Bingley did not do justice to his own disposition. You have shown him off now much more than he did himself." Darcy was delighted to have her enter the fray. He knew his other antagonist was already reeling, and would soon offer up his sword.

"I am exceedingly gratified," Bingley thanked her, "by your converting what my friend says into a compliment on the sweetness of my temper. But I am afraid you are giving it a turn which that gentleman did by no means intend; for he would certainly think the better of me, if under such a circumstance I were to give a flat denial, and ride off as fast as I could."

"Would Mr. Darcy then consider the rashness of your original intention as atoned for by your obstinacy in adhering to it?" Superbly done! thought Darcy; she takes the offensive with an admirable twist.

"Upon my word I cannot exactly explain the matter," said Bingley, somewhat at a loss in his attempt to follow the rapidity of Elizabeth's thought and turn it to advantage. "Darcy must speak for himself."

Into Hertfordshire

And Bingley falls out of the hunt, Darcy observed to himself in triumph—his advocate has passed him by in two sentences. "You expect me to account for opinions which you choose to call mine," he said, addressing himself to Elizabeth, "but which I have never acknowledged. Allowing the case, however, to stand according to your representation, you must remember, Miss Bennet, that the friend who is supposed to desire his return to the house, and the delay of his plan, has merely desired it, asked it without offering one argument in favour of its propriety."

"To yield readily—easily—to the *persuasion* of a friend is no merit with you?" she asked, fixing him with a stern eye, like a school mistress admonishing a young pupil. Darcy could not help noticing that she reserved this most playful side of her personality almost exclusively to himself. He was deeply gratified—touched and warmed, really—by her choosing to share with him this kind of intellectual intimacy. To her argument he replied: "To yield without conviction is no compliment to the understanding of either."

She made a circuit around his chair before facing him directly. Looking down on him, although perhaps not from as great a height as she might have wished, she took him to task: "You appear to me, Mr. Darcy, to allow nothing for the influence of friendship and affection. A regard for the requester would often make one readily yield to a request without waiting for arguments to reason one into it. I am not particularly speaking of such a case as you have supposed about Mr. Bingley. We may as well wait, perhaps, till the circumstance occurs, before we discuss the discretion of his behaviour thereupon. But in general and ordinary cases between friend and friend, where one of them is desired by the other to change a resolution of no very great moment, should you think ill of that person for complying with the desire, without waiting to be argued into it?"

All throughout this lecture Darcy's eyes were fixed on Elizabeth's; she had delighted him completely with both her charming air and well-reasoned attack. He now settled

Chapter XI

himself deeper into his chair with happy anticipation: this was meat and drink to him. "Will it not be advisable," said he with relish, "before we proceed on this subject, to arrange with rather more precision the degree of importance which is to appertain to this request, as well as the degree of intimacy subsisting between the parties?"

But Bingley here broke in on their discourse: "By all means, let us hear all the particulars, not forgetting their comparative height and size." Bingley knew the extremes to which his friend was capable of carrying this type of argument, now he had set his teeth in it, and contention of any kind was distressing to Bingley's feelings. "For that will have more weight in the argument, Miss Bennet, than you may be aware of. I assure you that if Darcy were not such a great tall fellow, in comparison with myself, I should not pay him half so much deference. I declare I do not know a more awful object than Darcy, on particular occasions, and in particular places; at his own house especially, and of a Sunday evening when he has nothing to do."

"Charles! How can you speak so of Mr. Darcy? You always talk such nonsense!" Miss Bingley cast an appalled look at Mr. Darcy for fear that he was as offended as she by her brother's incivility.

On his part, Darcy paused, then smiled ruefully as he recognised his friend's allusion to their dinner in London; Bingley was reminding him of his over-zealousness in seeking to win his point. Regretfully he lowered his shield and capitulated to his friend's wishes. "I see your design, Bingley," he acknowledged. "You dislike an argument, and want to silence this."

"Perhaps I do." He glanced from Darcy to Elizabeth and back, as though trying to assess their respective humours. "Arguments are too much like disputes. If you and Miss Bennet will defer yours till I am out of the room, I shall be very thankful; and then you may say whatever you like of me."

"What you ask is no sacrifice on my side," said Elizabeth, making Bingley a slight curtsey, "and Mr. Darcy had

Into Hertfordshire

much better finish his letter." In her response Darcy found more gentility and better manners than the more powerfully expressed disapprobation of Miss Bingley, which, if anything, lent Bingley's words more force, rather than softening them. Elizabeth kindly took upon herself the admonition to desist, thereby relieving him from his due share of the embarrassment. In this he saw a real concern for his interests and dignity; he could not be blind to that generous impulse that led her to sacrifice her dignity to spare his.

> I have been drawn off again, Dearest, by a most agreeable interlude. Miss Bingley began it with another commendation of my letter, and her brother, who is, I gather, just as tired as I am of her perpetual compliments, took the opportunity to get in a dig at me to balance matters up. Miss Bingley came to my defence immediately, and Miss Elizabeth Bennet took up Bingley's cause. I do not know where she was educated (surely not in Hertfordshire), but she is highly accomplished in debate and logic. She managed to turn a comment Bingley made on his untidy habits of thought into a testament to his humility. Now, Bingley has many excellent qualities, but on my honour, humility is not one of them: he is proud enough of his accomplishments—his natural modesty lies in the fact that he simply fails to recognise many of them. He would allow her interpretation to stand, however, being well-pleased to stand in borrowed glory. I returned his dig with interest, pointing out how deceitful false humility must be. I had him fairly cornered when his advocate came to his rescue. But she quickly outran his wit and he dropt out of the race, as his sister had done even earlier, leaving the two of us to finish the course; but, alas, in his amiability and the equanimity of his humour, Bingley does not

Chapter XI

appreciate the delights of active discourse, and felt Miss Elizabeth Bennet and I were perhaps too much in earnest in our dispute. He dissuaded me from continuing, drawing on his privilege as my friend to call a halt to the clash of our reasoning without the others' knowledge. I obliged him, of course: even if I did not hold him in such high regard, as a guest I could never be disobliging to my host; but I confess I have never been half so well entertained in this house before. Miss Elizabeth Bennet has dismissed me to "finish my letter," and so I shall, Dearest. I am hopeful of hearing from you soon, and I remain,
Your loving brother,
Fitzwilliam Darcy

After folding and sealing his letter, he sent his gaze around the room: Elizabeth had returned to her needlework; Hurst and Bingley were back at their game; Mrs. Hurst was alternately peering over her husband's shoulder and turning her jewellery about to observe the sparkle; and Miss Bingley sat looking blankly about her, obviously in want of occupation. Elizabeth, on the other hand, was a study in poise, grace, and feminine perfection where she sat bowed over her work. Again he was struck by the comparison of the two ladies; the one with all the advantages and none of the substance, the other with all the resources of heart and mind, but denied the fullest expansion of them by the condition of her family.

He became aware that his eyes had rested overlong on Elizabeth, and hastily looked away. His glance lit on the pianoforte, which brought to him the happy thought of asking her to play. In that way he would be satisfying himself on two counts: he would have the pleasure of her performance, and he could indulge himself in the observation of her without fear of offending. Of course, to single her out in this request would slight the other ladies, so instead he

Into Hertfordshire

spoke generally to the room, "Might we indulge in some music? Bingley, Hurst, you would not mind?"

The gentlemen waved him on, but Miss Bingley had got in ahead of him. She, having by that time already got to the pianoforte and opened it, hesitated just long enough to ask Elizabeth to precede her, before seating herself with the air of one who means to play forever. Miss Bennet murmured a polite negative, even though it was already apparent that her hostess had no thought of relinquishing her position at the instrument. Mrs. Hurst stepped over to join her sister, as the two ladies were fond of singing together, and they began a duet. Elizabeth returned to her work, but would look up now and again to observe the performance.

This arrangement was not to Darcy's liking. Miss Bingley was often looking his way to see how he was enjoying her recital, and it would be immediately obvious to her if he were to give his attention to Elizabeth. He therefore rose and stepped over to the fireplace, from which vantage point he could better observe Elizabeth, and at the same time stand slightly behind Miss Bingley. Elizabeth, however, chose that moment to put aside her work and wander over to the pianoforte to look through some of the music laying on it. Darcy was satisfied: he could now indulge in a modest observation of Elizabeth while seeming to attend the entertainment.

He held his post with perfect contentment through several selections, until Elizabeth, having perused the music books available, stepped to the end of the instrument and looked about the room. Her eyes caught his, and he was moved to take a step he had never before in his life undertaken: to ask a woman to dance because he wished to be near her.

Miss Bingley was at that moment playing a lively Scotch reel, which, of all dances, was Darcy's least favourite, but that seemed a minor obstacle to him now as, with slow and wondering step, he approached Elizabeth. Taking firm rein on his emotions and his manners, he asked, "Do

Chapter XI

not you feel a great inclination, Miss Bennet, to seize such an opportunity of dancing a reel?" He was amazed at his own voice speaking the words.

Elizabeth, however, made no reply. She turned her face up to him with a brief, pensive smile, then turned back to the performers. Darcy was surprised and perplexed: he knew she had heard him, but what was she playing at? For he was certain that this was yet another turn in their game of wits. Knowing from long observation, however, that teazing behaviour in a woman meant that its object had her approbation, he was encouraged to continue:

"I say, Miss Bennet," he repeated, "do not you feel the inclination to dance?"

"Oh! I heard you before," said she, "but I could not immediately determine what to say in reply. You wanted me, I know, to say 'Yes,' that you might have the pleasure of despising my taste; but I always delight in overthrowing those kind of schemes, and cheating a person of their premeditated contempt. I have, therefore, made up my mind to tell you, that I do not want to dance a reel at all—and now despise me if you dare."

Darcy quite nearly laughed out loud; she had diddled him properly. With no way either to agree with her or contend with her, he could only admit defeat, collect his wounded, and retire from the field. Smiling, he bowed and said respectfully, "Indeed, I do not dare."

Holding his delight to him like a rare gem, he sat down again to reflect on her performance. Never had his acquaintance been graced by a woman whose turn of mind gave him such pleasure. Never, in fact, had he met any one of either sex whose wit so closely complemented his own. And further, as he looked over at her where she again leaned on the pianoforte, the light of the fire highlighting her form, he had to admit that she had charms for him beyond those of wit and lively discourse. His delight turned slowly to a bemused wonderment: this must be how Bingley so often felt about *his* companions amongst the fair sex. If this were London instead of Hertfordshire, Darcy felt

Into Hertfordshire

he must be in some danger of losing his independence. He rather thought that if Elizabeth had possessed the standing and connections of the women who belonged to his acquaintance in Town, he would be in danger, indeed.

Chapter Twelve

The morning following his debate with Elizabeth, Darcy was forced to conclude that he must have been too obvious in his attentions to her, as Miss Bingley was more cutting than usual in her attempts at humour, and devoted a considerable amount of time to imagining and describing his future felicity with Elizabeth. She abused the Bennet family in more ways than Darcy could have imagined, at times even offending *him*, simply by the ill-spirited bent of her invective. Moreover, she and her sister were so uncivil to Miss Elizabeth Bennet that Darcy felt the sting of it more even than Elizabeth seemed to. It occurred to him for the first time that Miss Bingley might regard Elizabeth as a rival of some significance. This was absurd, to his mind, on two counts: first, Miss Bingley did not now possess, and never would possess, the power to attract his addresses; second, Elizabeth was entirely safe from his addresses, due to the insurmountable difficulties posed by her family. Notwithstanding the absurdity of Miss Bingley's misconception, he warned himself to be more guarded in future—he had no wish to cause Elizabeth pain: either directly, by raising any hopes of his own addresses, or indirectly, by exposing her to Miss Bingley's jealousy.

Finding himself in need of respite after a morning spent with Miss Bingley and the other inmates of the house, Darcy took himself off for a stroll in the shrubbery; he had not been out for a quarter-hour when Miss Bingley came to find him. "There you are, Mr. Darcy! Come out to enjoy the country air, have you? Once you are married, you will doubtless have many such walks with your dear bride, and her mother—and, of course, her younger sisters; —and the officers, too, I shouldn't wonder." She finished with a knowing laugh intended to charm.

Into Hertfordshire

"Miss Bingley," was Darcy's notably subdued response. "I am pleased you are here; I wished to tell you that, with your permission, I shall be spending the afternoon in my own rooms."

"You are not unwell, I hope?" asked Miss Bingley with real concern.

"No, no, I am quite well; merely...fatigued...and as I have some necessary business to attend to, I fear my energies would be too low to make me good company."

Miss Bingley linked her arm through his, saying, "Of course, — although you could never be unwelcome company, under any circumstances."

"I must also ask to be excused from this evening's entertainments, as I have some reading I promised myself I would attend to while here in Hertfordshire. I trust you — and Mr. Hurst — will take no offense?"

"Certainly not, I assure you. You must do just as you please, Mr. Darcy. I am sure none of us would mind in the least."

"I thank you." Darcy then attempted to release her arm from his, but the lady did not seem to notice, and continued walking along the path with him more or less in tow.

Looking about the countryside, she said, "Do you really not mind Country life then, Mr. Darcy? I should have thought you would find it excessively dull."

"I find that it is the people, not the place, who make for dull surroundings — or the reverse — Miss Bingley."

"Do you not find these people dull then, Sir? You must, I am sure. How you must long for your more sophisticated acquaintance in London, as do I."

"I confess that I have been happily surprised here; while nothing to brag about in general, I have found more here than I could have expected before our arrival." Miss Bingley studied him through carefully veiled eyes, but said nothing.

Darcy did not manage to escape until some time later, when Mrs. Hurst and Elizabeth joined them in their stroll; the party whole broke up shortly thereafter. On regaining

Chapter XII

the house, Darcy followed his avowed intentions, and spent the afternoon hours quietly in his rooms, attending to his affairs and his correspondence.

> Netherfield Hall, Herts.
> November 15, —
>
> Dear Edmund,
>
> Pray excuse my long silence, Cousin; one so often lets the days pile up without noticing. You will, I know, wish to hear how Georgiana does. She continues much as she has been, although I have recently detected a greater openness, which encourages me to hope that the worst is past.
>
> Thank you again, both for having gone out of your way to be at Pemberley, and for being so obliging as to leave it again so soon after your arrival. If it had been my first choice, you know I would rather you had stayed, but I did feel, and still do feel, that we ought to allow ourselves to be guided by Georgiana's wishes to a reasonable extent. She has written me again after an hiatus of over a month's time, and requested my correspondence; I hereby ask that you might also favour her with yours, even if she is dilatory in returning it. She holds you very dear, I know, Edmund, and she would be most gratified to receive your thoughts and good wishes.
>
> As for myself, I am finding Hertfordshire diverting; at least, more so than I had anticipated. Bingley's place, Netherfield Park, is a pleasant little estate, and the weather has been favourable for sport. The company here in the country is, as country neighbourhoods always are, rather limited, but still, it is more varied than we can hope for in Kent this Easter: fortify your spirits well this winter, Cousin, for you know what follows.
>
> I trust your duties in His Majesty's service are not too arduous, and that you are contriving

Into Hertfordshire

to keep the ladies of our acquaintance from pining overmuch for the want of male companionship until the Season opens. My plans for the Christmas holidays are unchanged; if yours are the same, then we shall look forward to seeing your esteemed parents, your brother (if events allow), and yourself, at Grosvenor Square on or about the nineteenth December.

Yours, &c.

Fitzwilliam Darcy

*****

Netherfield Hall
November 15, —

My dear Georgiana,

I have ensconced myself in my chambers this afternoon, as I feel a need for solitude not unlike your own. Even when one is genuinely fond of one's companions, there are times when nothing is better suited to a contemplative nature than a period of quietude and solitary repose. Little has changed since my letter yesterday, except, perhaps, that Miss Bingley has been more trying than usual. I have told you before that I suspected her of entertaining hopes of becoming mistress of Pemberley, and my stay in Hertfordshire has, if anything, added to that conviction. She has, on numerous occasions, attempted to increase the intimacy of our acquaintance to a degree I could never allow. I shall give you one example, although there have been many, as this instance struck me with particular force: on the occasion of an assembly here in the village, Miss Bingley actually sent her maid to Perkins with directions as to my attire, that I might match her own. I can im-

Chapter XII

agine your surprise at such impertinence, and I heartily agree—I was never more affronted; beyond that, however, I see in this presumption of privilege an attempt to persuade either herself, or me, or all parties concerned, that we are on terms. That I have never given any hint of willingness to be on terms with Miss Bingley goes without saying, yet here is my dilemma: how can I dissuade her and bring about a cessation of these intrigues and machinations without causing pain or offense to my friend? You know my feelings on deceit and the evils it brings: I hereby add guile and duplicity to the list of things I abhor.

In addition, it was borne in upon me to-day that Miss Bingley might harbour some feelings of jealousy with regard to myself; and towards Miss Elizabeth Bennet, of all people. I freely admit that I admire Miss Elizabeth Bennet's wit and humour, but there can never be more than that between us, obviously. The pain afforded to Miss Bingley by this jealousy would count for little, as it is of her own making, but she is disobliging and ill-mannered to Miss Elizabeth Bennet as well, which, to my mind, shows an unconscionable lack of good breeding. The manner in which ladies contest with their tongues I find most vexatious; although I will say that Miss Elizabeth Bennet never stoops to any such sign of ill-breeding—at least, she has never done so in my presence, and Miss Bingley has offered her numerous opportunities for such a display of pique. But perhaps I am too severe on my fellow creatures. Men are more formally civil than women in their dealings with one another, I believe, for among men harsh or disobliging words lead to anger and swift blows: the matter is either settled directly, or it may, in extreme cases, be necessary to resort to a challenge. But women, having no such ready release for their antipathies, must find other means of contestation. Or, looking at the same phenomenon from an entirely different viewpoint, perhaps we men are simply more easily offended than women, and in our contumacious natures we have no restraints to keep us from violence, so we practise civility the more diligently simply to keep ourselves from each other's throats. It is an interesting question, and I am sure it would take a wiser man than I to resolve it. What I do know with certainty is that if any man had behaved towards me the way Miss Bingley has towards Miss Elizabeth Bennet, I should have no alternative but to call him out.

The weather here has been seasonable and there has been some sport, but much of our time has been spent within doors. I am beginning to believe it is time that I thought of returning to London, and thence home to escort you to Grosvenor Square for the winter Season. Bingley contemplates giving a ball within a fortnight, so I have that much more reason to absent myself from Hertfordshire.

Well, I have, I believe, bored you with my small affairs long enough, and so I shall close, Dearest. Know that you are always in my thoughts, and that I remain,
Your loving brother,
Fitzwilliam Darcy

The weather had been unsettled all day, and now spits of cold rain were hitting the windows. After writing a short letter of instructions to his steward at Pemberley, Darcy spent the remainder of that quiet afternoon sitting before the fire, his thoughts drifting. They turned often to Elizabeth: wistfully, on his own behalf, but he was more deeply saddened for her sake, when thinking of the life she could look forward to. In his mind's eye he saw her as she might

Chapter XII

have become, had she been born to greater wealth and less exceptional relations: amongst the gaiety and variety of London, she might have become one of Society's leading lights, had she wished it, or found endless delight in its constantly changing society, its broad intellectual horizons, and its many diversions and entertainments; but this vision contrasted sharply with what he foresaw for her in her present circumstances, where her talents would be squandered on those of lesser abilities, and ground dull by drudgery and disuse. He passed the afternoon away thus, alternately watching the rain and wishing from his heart that things might be different—certainly for Elizabeth—and, perhaps, for himself too.

Chapter Thirteen

*D*inner was late that afternoon as Miss Bennet was to come down after dinner for the first time since her illness began, and Mrs. Hurst and Miss Bingley wished to give her ample time to prepare herself. When Darcy and the other gentlemen left the dining-room and repaired to the drawing-room, they found her warmly wrapt, with her sister and the other ladies in attendance on her. On his entering the room, Miss Bingley made an immediate play for his attention, greeting him with all the warmth at her command; he glanced her way in acknowledgement, but addressed himself instead to Miss Bennet with a bow, wanting to show Elizabeth the depth of his respect for her by honouring her sister with his best manners: "Miss Bennet, it is a great pleasure to see you well again. My sincere congratulations on your recovery." His eye glanced also upon Elizabeth to observe what her response might be to this bit of civility, but she had eyes only for her sister. He felt a tug inside at the tenderness and care that glowed in Elizabeth's eyes as she attended the invalid. Hurst, with his usual sensibility, merely bowed in passing to Miss Bennet as he sought the sideboard and a bit of honey-cake. Bingley, however, could scarcely contain his joy.

"My dear Miss Bennet," cried he, "thank the Lord you are better! You gave us all quite a turn, you know; we were *so* very worried! And here you are, recovered at last. But come, you must move over by the fire. I am afraid you are too close to the door; the draughts are not good for you." Miss Bennet obligingly rose, and, with the help of her sister, and many cautions and words of concern from Bingley, sat in a chair on the other side of the room next to the hearth. Darcy followed them with his eyes.

Catching Miss Bingley's eyes upon him, he turned from the group by the fire and fetched himself a measured

Chapter XIII

amount of port wine. From behind him he heard Bingley observe to Miss Bennet: "Do you know, it has been nine days since I have seen you? Not since Sir William's party. It seems *such* a frightfully long time!" Bingley had always had a curiously exact memory for dates, a trait Darcy had sometimes wondered at, for, in general, his friend's memory was not such a paragon of reliability.

Taking his glass, he sat down unobtrusively in a corner. His mood was still upon him, and he asked nothing better than a deep chair in a quiet corner with his book. Hurst sat down at the card table and called out to Miss Bingley, "Well now, my dear sister, shall we have a go? Name your pleasure; I feel in luck this evening." However, Miss Bingley, knowing that Darcy had no thought of playing at cards this evening, declined this invitation. "My dear Mr. Hurst, I fear you will find no one to test your luck this evening; and as you always manage to best *me*, no matter what your luck might be, I shall not be sorry for it." Hurst then enquired of the company at large, and was met with a disappointingly uniform silence. His philosophy was sufficient to meet this exigence, however: he, with great fortitude in the face of misfortune, fetched a generous glass of wine and arrayed himself on a sofa in preparation for a communion with Morpheus.

Darcy, having been thus released from all companionable duties, took up his book for the evening: a learned work by Mr. Adam Smith on the source of a nation's wealth, very much discussed among those concerned with such matters, as it presented novel thinking on how capital might be increased. Darcy had been introduced to the work at Oxford, but had not thought seriously on it until he had assumed the responsibilities of managing the family's affairs on his father's death; then it had taken on a more important claim on his attention. Darcy took his duties as landlord very seriously and constantly sought for ways to improve the condition of his tenants and his lands. He was attempting, once again, to reconcile Smith's postulate that labour, not land, was the driving force of a nation's econo-

Into Hertfordshire

my, with his own circumstances. If Smith's postulate was correct, how did one maximise return on a landed estate? Was the land raw material for the labour, and would the principle of division of labour function as Smith proposed? And how, then, was the labour to be properly divided? Darcy made a point to spend time on such questions every term, as he believed that Smith's "invisible hand," by which individuals were guided to increase society's wealth and health through the pursuit of their own interests, should and must be felt more keenly and consciously by those possessed of wealth. His ancestors, he supposed, would have called this *noblesse oblige*, but in Darcy's estimation the rational self-interest expounded by Smith seemed a sturdier reed than a disinterested wish to do good for others.

Miss Bingley, seeking to find interest in his studies, had picked up the second volume of the book, which had given Darcy a good deal of amusement at first; but when she began asking question after question he found his amusement waning. Some questions, however, had their own unintentional humour, as when she asked: "By 'domestic industry,' I assume he means needlework and the like—or does he refer to servants' duties?" As was often the case during an evening with Miss Bingley, Darcy's tongue was well-bitten before it was over.

Fortunately, her interest in the subject was exhausted early, and she contrived to abandon that activity with the observation: "How pleasant it is to spend an evening in this way! I declare after all there is no enjoyment like reading! How much sooner one tires of anything than of a book! When I have a house of my own, I shall be miserable if I have not an excellent library." Having thus gracefully excused herself from the activity, she discarded the book carelessly onto the sideboard while selecting a cake; Darcy winced at this abuse of a book, for he held a scholar's reverence for the written word, but he bit still more deeply into his already scourged tongue and was silent. Indeed, recognising the signs that she was now moving on to another pastime, he sunk lower in his armchair in the hopes that her

Chapter XIII

new diversion, whatever it might be, would not involve him.

He was left in peace, however, for at that moment Miss Bingley overheard something of her brother's conversation with Miss Bennet, and entered into it by saying, "By the bye, Charles, are you really serious in meditating a dance at Netherfield? I would advise you, before you determine on it, to consult the wishes of the present party; I am much mistaken if there are not some among us to whom a ball would be rather a punishment than a pleasure."

"If you mean Darcy," said he with a good-natured gibe at his friend, "he may go to bed, if he chooses, before it begins—but as for the ball, it is quite a settled thing; and as soon as Nicholls has made white soup enough, I shall send round my cards." Bingley arched a challenging brow at Darcy, but he disdained to reply. Raising his book a little higher, he scowled at the page in a most convincing show of studiousness.

"I should like balls infinitely better," Miss Bingley observed, "if they were carried on in a different manner; but there is something insufferably tedious in the usual process of such a meeting. It would surely be much more rational if conversation, instead of dancing, were made the order of the day." She looked towards Darcy with a secretive little nod, to show him how closely their thoughts coincided on the importance of matters of intellect over mere social forms. He turned a page, unimpressed by this parade of what he knew to be a very lately developed devotion to the pleasures of the mind.

After casting about some minutes for another means of engaging Darcy's attention, Miss Bingley began to walk about the room, in hopes that he, like other men before him, might not be insensitive to her figure, and elegance in movement. To Darcy, though he might not be insensible to such charms, this inducement was stale through custom; and further, he had absolutely no intention of attending to Miss Bingley's personal charms in the presence of Elizabeth. His eyes staid fixed on his book.

Into Hertfordshire

Miss Bingley completed one languid turn about the room, gracing various objects by allowing her fingers to drape and caress them as she passed by, but still she failed to arouse Darcy's attention. Finally, she essayed one last, impulsive stratagem: "Miss Eliza Bennet, let me persuade you to follow my example, and take a turn about the room. I assure you it is very refreshing after sitting so long in one attitude."

Darcy was surprised at hearing this, and Elizabeth appeared no less so, but politely acceded to the request. This, at last, caught Darcy's attention, and he watched the two of them while puzzling over this sudden rapprochement. Had Miss Bingley given over her jealousy and contention with Elizabeth? But as soon as she perceived that his attention had lifted from his studies, Miss Bingley immediately invited him to join them; this explained it: she merely wished to draw him out of his book, using Elizabeth to bait the snare. If he were to join them, she would instantly abandon her. On the point of declining, he was struck by a sudden, mischievous impulse: "I can imagine, Miss Bingley," said he in answer to her invitation, "only two motives for your choosing to walk about the room in this manner, and with either of which my joining you would interfere."

The two ladies stopped their amble to regard Darcy. "What could he mean, Miss Eliza?" demanded Miss Bingley. "I am dying to know his meaning! Can you understand him at all?"

"Not at all," answered she; "but depend upon it, he means to be severe on us, and our surest way of disappointing him will be to ask nothing about it."

Darcy had hoped Elizabeth would rise to the bait, but he was unconcerned by her answer, knowing that Miss Bingley surely would not be able to let it lie. He favoured them with an assured and mildly provoking smile. As he had known she would, Miss Bingley insisted on receiving an explanation of the two motives he ascribed to them. When her entreaties at length subsided, he replied, "I have not the smallest objection to explaining them. You either

Chapter XIII

choose this method of passing the evening because you are in each other's confidence, and have secret affairs to discuss, or because you are conscious that your figures appear to the greatest advantage in walking; if the first, I should be completely in your way, and if the second, I can admire you much better as I sit by the fire."

"Oh! shocking!" cried Miss Bingley, with a delighted smile. "I never heard anything so abominable. How shall we punish him for such a speech?"

Darcy had noticed Elizabeth's eyes widen in surprise at his words, and felt his ploy to be a success. But she soon found the upper hand: "Nothing so easy, if you have but the inclination," she replied to Miss Bingley. "We can all plague and punish one another. Teaze him—laugh at him. Intimate as you are, you must know how it is to be done."

Darcy's eyes narrowed and he brought his mind fully alert, for he sensed battle in the offing. To be the butt of humour was what Darcy always sought to avoid: as master of Pemberley, he felt it his duty to hold himself beyond the reach of such impertinence, and, as he was proud to be who he was, he felt such mockery to be a personal affront; he had no wish to expose himself to such in front of Elizabeth, and even less desire to receive it from her.

Miss Bingley was, of course, disinclined to take the field against him. "But upon my honour I do *not*," said she. "I do assure you that my intimacy has not yet taught me *that*. Teaze calmness of temper and presence of mind! No, no—I feel he may defy us there. And as to laughter, we will not expose ourselves, if you please, by attempting to laugh without a subject. Mr. Darcy may hug himself."

"Mr. Darcy is not to be laughed at!" Elizabeth protested. "That is an uncommon advantage, and uncommon I hope it will continue, for it would be a great loss to *me* to have many such acquaintances. I dearly love a laugh."

Darcy, for the moment believing himself to be on safe ground, and interested, as always, in Elizabeth's thoughts, made this cautious reply: "Miss Bingley has given me credit for more than can be. The wisest and the best of men—nay,

Into Hertfordshire

the wisest and best of their actions—may be rendered ridiculous by a person whose first object in life is a joke."

"Certainly," agreed Elizabeth, "there are such people, but I hope I am not one of *them*. I hope I never ridicule what is wise or good. Follies and nonsense, whims and inconsistencies, *do* divert me, I own, and I laugh at them whenever I can. But these, I suppose, are precisely what you are without."

Darcy smiled slightly at such a trap. Human frailties are universal, and only a man wonderfully ignorant of his own nature could claim otherwise. Did she think him so foolish as to fall for such an obvious trick? Springes to catch woodcocks! "Perhaps that is not possible for any one," he disavowed gently. "But it has been the study of my life to avoid those weaknesses which often expose a strong understanding to ridicule."

"Such as vanity and pride," suggested Elizabeth archly.

Though her air was light-hearted, Darcy gave her words serious consideration. Vanity? No, he was not vain. But he *was* proud, there was no denying it: proud of his accomplishments; proud of his natural abilities; and even, a little, proud of being Darcy of Pemberley—it had cost him no little effort to become that individual, after all. He was aware that he appeared to some to be *too* proud, but he did not feel himself to be guilty of an arrogant conceit; it was merely that he was, in his own mind, justifiably particular in choosing his intimates, and that he made a very clear distinction between his behaviour with his intimates and his behaviour among the rest of society. Further, his philosophy held that only the opinions of oneself held by those with whom one was intimate could be worthy of acknowledgement, as the rest of the world formed their opinions from ignorance; therefore, the uninformed opinions of the world at large held no more sway with him than his did with them—this was not arrogance, just human nature. That people in general thought him arrogant troubled him not at all, since he knew this was just a mistaken impres-

Chapter XIII

sion. And where an arrogant man sees no faults in himself, Darcy was perfectly aware that his nature harboured a reasonably complete catalogue of them. Understanding begins with oneself, after all. "Yes," he replied at length, "vanity is a weakness indeed. But pride—where there is a real superiority of mind, pride will be always under good regulation."

At this Elizabeth turned away from him, but whether from vexation, or amusement, or even just to gain time to prepare her next attack, he could not tell.

"Your examination of Mr. Darcy is over," said Miss Bingley, "and pray what is the result?"

"I am perfectly convinced by it that Mr. Darcy has no defect. He owns it himself without disguise."

To this point Darcy had enjoyed their game, but he now felt he owed Elizabeth—no; he wished to give her—not mere wit, but something of greater depth. Watching her carefully for any sign of misunderstanding, he demurred: "No, I have made no such pretension. I have faults enough, but they are not, I hope, of understanding. My temper I dare not vouch for. It is, I believe, too little yielding—certainly too little for the convenience of the world. I cannot forget the follies and vices of others so soon as I ought, nor their offences against myself. My feelings are not puffed about with every attempt to move them. My temper would perhaps be called resentful. My good opinion once lost, is lost forever."

"*That* is a failing indeed!" cried Elizabeth. "Implacable resentment *is* a shade in a character. But you have chosen your fault well. I really cannot *laugh* at it. You are safe from me."

Darcy was less interested in being safe from Elizabeth than in being understood by her. Her playful astonishment gave Darcy to know that she had not recognised that he had left their teazing game of wits behind, so he tried again: "There is, I believe, in every disposition a tendency to some particular evil—a natural defect, which not even the best education can overcome."

Into Hertfordshire

"And *your* defect is a propensity to hate everybody," she accused with mock severity.

Not at all, thought Darcy to himself; only a propensity to love very few. But now, let us have a little truth about you, Miss Elizabeth Bennet. "And yours," he retorted, although he smiled as he spoke, "is wilfully to misunderstand them."

Miss Bingley, who had been listening to their exchange with growing alarm—recognising the fact that Darcy had never addressed her with such candour—decided that a diversion was necessary, instantly. "Do let us have a little music!" she cried. "Louisa, you will not mind my waking Mr. Hurst?" The pianoforte was opened hurriedly and a rather loud piece begun with spirit. Elizabeth curtseyed to Darcy with an enigmatic smile and returned to her seat.

Darcy watched her receding back regretfully. Elizabeth had not appreciated his honesty for what it was, and this disappointed him. He was certain it was simply a lack of recognition of his change of purpose, and not a deliberate snub; notwithstanding, he wished it had turned out better. He looked with resentment at Miss Bingley, for it was her intrusion into their discussion that had cut off his attempt to reach an improved understanding between Elizabeth and himself.

When his thoughts arrived at this point, however, he brought himself up short. What, exactly, did he mean by such an endeavour? He never spoke in this unguarded fashion with any one other than his sister. When, precisely, had Elizabeth—that is, Miss Elizabeth Bennet—reached such an elevated status?

The more he considered, the more he came to realise how seriously he had over-stepped himself with regard to Miss Elizabeth Bennet. Upon reviewing his relations with her, it was evident that each time he spoke with her he became more sensible of the attraction of her wit and her person; unless he wished to give himself over to her powers altogether, it must end. Indeed, he must not do to Elizabeth—*Miss Elizabeth Bennet*—the very thing he had

Chapter XIII

reprimanded Bingley for doing to Miss Grantley, and since an alliance with the Bennet family was not faintly possible, he must cease his attentions to this member of it, no matter how charming he might find her. He sat for some time facing this realization, and its inescapable conclusion. Bingley's plaintive, "But I liked her!" echoed in his mind, but he firmly pushed the thought away. In this instance his likes and dislikes did not enter into the matter. Clearly, his superior position made it incumbent upon him to protect Elizabeth—*Miss Elizabeth Bennet!*—and to do so he must not allow her to feel that she might be able to influence his felicity. Regretfully, but with a strong conviction of rectitude, he returned to his book with a deep sense of purpose. If his eyes did wander from time to time in her direction, it could be for no other reason than to reassure himself of the correctness and necessity of his decision.

Chapter Fourteen

*M*iss Darcy read and reread her brother's last letter with an amused and wondering interest. Never in all her life had she known him to devote an entire letter to his relations with women; he rarely went so far as to mention a name, and then, more often than not, only that he might specifically draw her shortcomings to his sister's attention. Furthermore, he had made no reference at all to the burden under which she herself laboured. Very clearly, to her eyes at least, he found himself embroiled in an emotional tempest of a sort he had never experienced before. This was extremely intriguing to Georgiana; all the more so because she had always hoped to find a true friend and sister through her brother's marriage. There was no one in their Derbyshire acquaintance, nor yet in their London circle, with whom she shared any bond of affection, and she longed in her heart for such a friend. She knew, given her brother's character, that any woman who married him for the right reasons would possess a most warm and caring nature, in order to see past his manner and into his heart, and a degree of understanding unusual among her sex, in order to have attracted him and earned his approbation. This gave her to cherish the hope that she might find in such a woman the friend of her heart she longed for. Miss Elizabeth Bennet, it appeared from his letters, had all this and more, and, to a sister's eye, his letters made it clear that he was already closer to an attachment than he had ever been before. A review of his previous letters showed nothing to injure this conclusion.

Her own troubled heart was eased considerably by imagining her brother happily married. She had come close at times to believing him too much alone, as he always seemed to stand outside of his circle and observe it, rather than to be a part of it—and might have been inclined to believed it the more had she not been restrained by her

Chapter XIV

respect for him from presuming to pass judgment on his actions. His letters to her in the past were filled with his observations and opinions on his acquaintance, but rarely gave her to feel that he had any real partiality, aside from Mr. Bingley, for those who peopled his world. His manner of speaking of Miss Elizabeth Bennet, therefore, captured her attention most particularly. He had said that he admired her countenance, so she must be pretty; not too pretty, she hoped, for she knew that he had spurned women who were renowned for their form and features. Was Miss Bennet a Helen of Troy, then, to have thus drawn his interest? She considered it, but decided at length to believe otherwise; he spoke rather more of her mind and heart than of her appearance. She was pleased with this conclusion, as she had no desire to find herself related to a woman with such perfection of form; and she had rather that her brother's love have as its foundation the less superficial aspects of his beloved's nature. His own description of her had been "sincere", "witty", "charming", and "warm", as well as "amiable" and "modest"; had she set out to list those attributes most desirable in his wife and her sister, it could not have differed greatly from this. She could not understand, however, why he should object to her family. That he might wish to avoid so hazardous an undertaking as falling in love, she could understand—that was common enough amongst his sex; but he was so completely rational and honest that she could hardly imagine that he could so deceive himself with regard to his true motives as to hide them behind false objections. She resolved to do what was in her power to relieve his mind and minimise whatever difficulties he was imagining.

Miss Bingley, on the other hand, presented a real and immediate problem. While a description of her character would be very different from that for Miss Elizabeth Bennet, she was by no means a bad sort of person—but she was a most determined one. Georgiana could well imagine that she might finally achieve her goal simply by dint of her determination. Well, her brother had left open an enquiry as to what he might best do about her, and Georgiana had been privy to a side of her about which he might have need of knowing.

> Pemberley,
> November 17, —
>
> Dearest Fitzwilliam,
>
> Thank you for your letter of the 15th; I find your descriptions of what passes at Netherfield a most welcome diversion. What you write about Miss Bingley, unfortunately, does not surprise me as much as it should; in all truth I must confess that I have found in her an unfortunate tendency towards assurance, self-indulgence, and a certain coarseness of feeling; I hope you will forgive me for speaking so of some one of your acquaintance, but I believe this to be a very serious matter, and I would have you know what I know. I have heard her speaking with her sister in unguarded moments when there were no members of the opposite sex present, and observed in her a most...pragmatic...view of men. She counts herself amongst the most eligible women in London Society, and she is bent on making a "conquest worthy of her qualities," to use her expression; it would appear that she finds you worthy. I need hardly say, Brother, but be most circumspect. She is capable of ploys that make me blush to contemplate. Time, and an adherence to absolute propriety, will eventually discourage her, as she knows that youth is fleeting, and desires to make her "conquest" before her bloom is gone.
>
> But let me pass on to a more agreeable topic: I am most desirous of knowing more of Miss Elizabeth Bennet; what you have written interests me greatly. Brother, you have confused me exceedingly, for you say on the one hand that she is all that is amiable, and on the other that any connec-

Chapter XIV

tion with her family is unthinkable; yet you have never said *why*. As you know, I am forced to conclude that she is a gentleman's daughter, by her inclusion in the Netherfield family circle. What, then, is the impediment? You have mentioned her nonsensical mother, but it cannot be this, because, well...Good Heavens, if one were to name all of the nonsensical mothers in London, or in Derbyshire, for that matter—and most certainly in Kent—the list would be formidable, indeed.

And I am very troubled to hear that you will leave before the ball; pray do not—please? We shall be amply prepared for our relations' visit without your hurrying your departure. Will you not stay to dance with Miss Elizabeth Bennet? I would have you do so, dear Brother, truly I would. It would be a shame indeed if you were to lose her acquaintance forever without ever once having danced with her.

I have already begun preparations for our removal to Town. Mrs. Annesley and I have discussed what is needful, and have already planned several possible entertainments for the time our family is all together; so you see, Fitzwilliam, there is no need for you to hurry your return.

I shall hope to hear that you have changed your mind, and decided to stay, when I receive your next letter.

Your affectionate sister,
Georgiana Darcy

Chapter Fifteen

*T*he morning after his unhappy illumination regarding his feelings and obligations towards Miss Elizabeth Bennet, Darcy heard that the Bennet ladies were to return home on the day following; he met the news with a mixture of regret and relief. He knew himself well enough to know that, once he had arrived at a conclusion, there could be no second thoughts: that he must relinquish Miss Elizabeth Bennet's acquaintance did not admit a doubt. Yet the difficulty of maintaining a proper distance from her would be very trying under their current circumstances. In the presence of the others at breakfast, where there was no want of conversation, he had no difficulty in maintaining his self-command; his mannerly resolve was sorely tested at one point later in the morning, however, as he was seated in the library before the Netherfield ledgers. She came in search of something to read, but beyond the introductory civilities, neither of them spoke for the half-an-hour or more she remained there. Darcy congratulated himself on his success, and his confidence in his strength increased; he was curiously aware, however, of the scent of flowers that followed her about and lingered even long after she was gone; and, unaccountably, he was able to get very little forward with his work. At length he gave up on the tallies and figures and went out of doors to clear his mind. Upon re-entering the Hall he exerted his vigilance for the remainder of the day, and, by the simple expedience of being constantly aware of Elizabeth's whereabouts, contrived never to be alone with her again. He thereby managed to regain his chambers in the evening without having spoken a dozen words to her altogether throughout the day: he again congratulated himself on having held so firmly to his resolve. He wrote to his sister, relating how he had spent his day, but, upon review, the letter seemed to

Chapter XV

convey the idea that he had done nothing other than follow Miss Elizabeth Bennet about the Hall all day. He therefore re-wrote it, giving what he deemed to be a more accurate, albeit brief, summation of his activities, and focused in the main on their plans for the Christmas holidays.

The next day was Sunday, and following Morning Services the two Bennet ladies left Netherfield. Miss Bennet smiled sweetly on one and all as she bid them adieu, thanking every one most sincerely for the many kindnesses she had received. Bingley, ever solicitous, made sure she was well supplied with rugs and warm bricks to fortify her against the rigours and inclemency of her three-mile journey back to Longbourn. Miss Elizabeth Bennet seemed in fine spirits at their departure; Darcy wondered at her joy in returning to her mother, but, after all, home is home, and must take precedence in the heart over any other place. Darcy hardly knew how to be sad they were gone, yet he watched their carriage longer than any one else in the party save Bingley himself. The two men turned and walked into the house together, though neither found anything to say to the other.

Chapter Sixteen

*T*he following Wednesday, Miss Darcy had been occupied in the early portion of the morning going over her brother's letters once again. In each one she could discover evidence of an increasing attraction for Miss Elizabeth Bennet. In his first he had dwelt at length on her own concerns, and she had been mentioned only in one brief line—although that line had been sufficiently marked in its approval of her as to have caught Georgiana's particular attention, even at the time. In the second, however, she saw such remarkable distinction of Miss Elizabeth Bennet as to quite amaze her. And by the third he made no mention of her own cares at all; it was nothing but his attitudes and actions regarding Miss Elizabeth Bennet and Miss Bingley. Never, *never* had she seen her brother thus absorbed in his relations with women, even briefly, and she was certain that his being so vexed with Miss Bingley was no more than the reflection of his regard for Miss Elizabeth Bennet; it was her presence that made him so aware of Miss Bingley's impertinence and importunities, and the injury done Miss Elizabeth Bennet by her jealous behaviour was what had brought into importance Miss Bingley's feelings towards himself.

Taken all together, she was persuaded that her brother was in a fair way to being in love, and that persuasion did more than months of repentance and solitude had done to unburden her heart. Having this object to think of and plan for had, without her realising, quite nearly removed the man who betrayed her from her thoughts. Her great desire for a sister and friend, in whom she could confide and share the daily affairs of her own sex, was forming itself more and more around the vision she had created of Miss Elizabeth Bennet, and had quite set aside her own cares. She read and re-read every line in which her brother spoke of her, trying

Chapter XVI

to divine from the very shape of his script every last scrap of meaning and intelligence about a woman who might, perhaps, become that sister and friend. In so doing she found two things to trouble her: why did she refuse to dance with him, and, most distressingly, why was he so insistent that there could be no alliance with her?

That he should wish to dance with her was, on the face of it, an obvious sign of the acuteness of his interest; she was well aware that he rarely danced, and then only with some one of close and long-standing acquaintance. She could not bring to mind any occasion on which he had willingly engaged the hand of a lady he had known weeks only. Miss Elizabeth Bennet, of course, could hardly know this, and so the distinction would be lost on her, but still—why should she refuse him? Miss Darcy was aware that her brother was wont to occasionally speak his mind without thought for those around him. That he might have in some way offended her unconsciously was a disturbing possibility, but Georgiana could not see how it might be remedied, or, indeed, how she might even ascertain it had occurred, without offending her brother in turn, by asking if he might have done so.

As to the second matter of concern, that he was so opposed to the idea of an alliance, she could see no compelling support for his conclusion, that the Bennets could not be accepted as relations; she poured over his letters again and again, searching in vain for the reason. The mother, certainly, did not sound desirable, but this she could not view as sufficient reason to deny the possibility of liaison between their families; Georgiana, even in her limited experience, knew that few families could boast of being free of provoking relations. Her own aunt, Lady Catherine, was as difficult and unreasonable as any one she could imagine, yet no one could take exception to her as a connection. No, she was persuaded rather that her brother was raising barriers on purpose to prevent his emotions from influencing him; he, who so resolutely held that the intellect alone ought to govern one's life, was not one to let his feelings gain ascendancy over him. In his last letter he had taken particular care to mention that he had gone through an entire day without having spoken to Miss Elizabeth Bennet at all; this, she was convinced, was exactly what he would do if he felt his sentiments beginning to overset his more rational faculties.

She had still another concern. In earlier letters he had made mention of the possibility of his returning home before Mr. Bingley's ball, but in this last letter he had spoken of it with more certainty; this was disturbing in the extreme. The only way Georgiana could see that he might finally be led in the direction of his best interests and her wishes was if he were to be exposed to Miss Elizabeth Bennet's company long enough for her charms to overcome his habitual distrust of his sensibilities. She must somehow convince him to remain.

She had just reached this conclusion when a knock at the door announced Mrs. Annesley. The good lady smiled at the papers spread about Miss Darcy on the sofa and observed: "You are making quite a study of those letters, Miss Darcy, dear. I had not known before that Hertfordshire was such a captivating destination. Is your brother's visit there so fascinating, then?"

Miss Darcy smiled in return, saying, "In some ways, it is, indeed. But only to a sister's heart; to no one else would they hold such interest." She folded them up and tucked them away in the desk.

"Well, then, you will be glad of this," said Mrs. Annesley, drawing forth a letter from her pocket. "It is from Mr. Darcy."

Georgiana rose instantly and went to take it from her. "Oh, thank you, Mrs. Annesley! I had hoped there might be something in the morning post."

"You are very fortunate to have a brother who is such a dependable correspondent; I do not think many sisters could boast of such."

"I am indeed; and that is the least of his goodness. Their contents are more valuable still."

Chapter XVI

"They certainly seem to have done you good, my dear; you seem happier now than at any time since I came into Derbyshire. If his letters be the cause, then I pray that his stay in Hertfordshire will be a long one." She smiled again and quietly left the room.

Miss Darcy, somewhat surprised at this comment, decided on reflection that it was true; indeed, she had not thought of her troubles, or her betrayer, all morning. While still wondering that this should be true, she hastily opened the seal.

> Netherfield
> November 17, —
>
> Dearest Georgiana,
>
> I am rather fatigued, as the time to-day seemed to drag on interminably, so this will be shorter than I might wish. The Misses Bennet left us to-day after Morning Services, and the effort to maintain a decent level of conversation in their absence has been painfully great. Bingley was, of course, much saddened by Miss Bennet's departure, which left his spirits low. Miss Bingley, on the other hand, was in very high spirits indeed after they left, but her conversation I found to be monotonous, as she never wavered from heaping scorn and abuse on her two erstwhile guests.
>
> Will it surprise you, Dearest, if I tell you that I found myself on the verge of an attraction for Miss Elizabeth Bennet? It is true. But be assured; I may have loosed the reins, but I did not fall off. I was most careful to shield her from any knowledge of my interest; I never even took her hand for a dance—no, that is not entirely accurate: rather, I would have to admit that she never accepted my hand for a dance—but perhaps I might have mentioned that before. In any event, she is gone, and I am reasonably well assured that she has no idea of having ever excited my esteem.

Into Hertfordshire

I must say, though, now she is no longer before me, that it has occurred to me to wonder at the fact that, after so many Seasons in London, the only woman ever to have captured my attention should be so impossibly distant from me in standing. Why, of the literally hundreds of women to whom I have been introduced, should the only one whose acquaintance is worth the having—for me, personally, that is—be so little esteemed in the eyes of Society? It puzzles me; upon my honour, it does puzzle me.

I have put any feelings I might have harboured for her behind me, of course. I could not in honour, in civility, in faith, distinguish her at all—there could be no hope of an alliance, and such regard as I may have had for her served no purpose other than to bring discomfort to the bearer of them. I own, however, that it has long appeared to me that the impish sports of Fate seem peculiarly to conspire against the wishes of men, giving us glimpses only of what felicity might be, then arranging the world so that no such happy lot can ever be ours. But come, I must not be self-pitying: I doubt not that there are very few in the whole of England who would feel that Darcy of Pemberley was in need of sympathy; one must always keep one's perspective.

Bingley, as I mentioned, was downcast (for him, that is) by the departure of Miss Bennet, but he has cheered himself with thoughts of the ball he plans this Tuesday week. With this diversion to occupy him, and with the expectation of dancing a set—or might we suspect that he intends to dance even more than one?—with the beguiling Miss Bennet, he will have no trouble supporting his spirits. I have not yet spoken to him, but I do not intend to stay to it; there would be no purpose and I would just as soon begin my journey to

Chapter XVI

Pemberley. My current plans are to leave this Saturday for Town, then set off for home next Tuesday week, as I mentioned before. I am counting the days until I shall be with you again.
Your loving—and homeward turning—brother,
Fitzwilliam Darcy

Georgiana's feelings, on reading this letter, were affected with such pressing urgency that she instantly sat down to compose her reply. A quick calculation told her that a letter sent that day would arrive just after his departure from Netherfield on the coming Saturday, so it was imperative that her letter be sent express that very day.

Pemberley
November 20, —

Dearest Fitzwilliam,

Have no fear, Brother, on receiving this letter by express, lest it contain ill-tidings; all is well here at Pemberley. It is only that I read with great disappointment in your last that you are definitely planning to leave Netherfield before Mr. Bingley's ball, and I was compelled to write you before this plan should be carried out. Why must you leave without attending the ball, Fitzwilliam? The idea that you will leave Miss Elizabeth Bennet behind you without ever having danced with her, quite breaks my heart. At the very least you must allow yourself to take her hand for one dance.

You see, as it happens, I was not so very surprised by the intelligence you offered in your letter, to the effect that you had found yourself attracted to Miss Elizabeth Bennet; inasmuch as she is the only lady you have ever distinguished to me by any degree of approbation, and since you have so distinguished her in each one of your letters since you met her, your admission comes too late for surprise. All that you have written to me of her has quite delighted me, Fitzwilliam, and I wish most earnestly to meet her. But, as you will know when you have received my earlier letters, I am at a loss to understand your objections to her. Surely her family's standing cannot be so far beneath our own as to forbid you even to feel for her, or she would never be admitted as a guest into Mr. Bingley's house. I would never presume to think you mistaken, but I would most sincerely wish to understand your thoughts more fully. And I hope you will forgive the question, my dear Brother, but are you sure that in deciding this you have also listened to your heart? That the heart and mind must always follow the same pole-star is not true, of course; but neither does it follow that the path chosen by the heart is *always* the wrong one.

But never mind *my* opinions on *your* heart; they mean little enough, indeed — you recently entreated me, though, to tell you if there was anything whatever that would give me pleasure, and I now ask this of you, Fitzwilliam: to gratify *my* heart, would you please stay to the ball, and dance with Miss Elizabeth Bennet? Please, for my sake? I can hardly explain why it should be so, but this means a great deal to me, and I do hope you will find it in your power to indulge me in this.

Your loving sister,
Georgiana Darcy

That it was daring of her to make such a request, she knew; but she told herself that it was in his best interest. As soon as it was finished, she hurriedly sealed it and rushed out to put it in the hands of Reynolds, the butler, not wishing to trust a footman with so pressing an affair. She impressed upon him that there must be no delay in sending it, and he promised to post it in the village himself within

Chapter XVI

the hour. Having done thus much, she could do no more than give way to anxious introspection, and enjoy all the benefits that usually accrue to those who worry about things beyond their control.

Chapter Seventeen

*D*arcy and his friend spent much of their time out of doors in the days following the removal of the Bennet sisters, as the unalloyed company within was not best suited to the mood of either. Darcy had at least had the pleasure of receiving two return letters from his sister. In the first it was clear that she still suffered, and in his reply he offered her what comfort and advice he could, but, in truth, it was difficult for him to find any way to soften the cold fact that such men as Wickham were to be found in the world. The best he could do was to point out that a signal function of one's family was to help one recover from being savaged by such predators. That, and the equally undeniable fact that men like Bingley were also to be found, whose great good-will and amiability were, in some measure, a counter-balance to the evils embodied by the Wickhams of the world.

But on Tuesday morning, the letter he received was a surprise to him; parts of it he might have written himself. She began the letter, which was the reply to the one written with Miss Bingley's kind assistance, by apologising again for her transgression, and then thanking him once more for his goodness to her; Darcy shook his head over this: he simply could not get her to accept her own worth, and the importance of the rôle she played in his life. But she then spoke so collectedly of her trials at Wickham's hands, and gave such a rational and reasoned analysis of how those trials had made it so difficult to trust again, that Darcy had to think back over his own letters of the last year or more, to reassure himself that she was not simply offering him back his own thoughts. At one point she wrote: "...I know wherein lies my mistake—what I do not know is how I can ever come to trust my feelings again. If the deepest feelings of one's heart can be so much in error, what hope is there of

Chapter XVII

ever finding contentment in life?" This expressed one of his own great philosophical dilemmas from the last winter. That the heart was a poor guide through life was every where demonstrated; he need look no further than his own family circle to find evidence, as neither his father's nor his sister's good hearts had kept them safe from Wickham. But how was one to find a woman to love with the mind, as well as the heart? To love with the heart was merely improbable; compounded by the near impossibility of deeply and truly esteeming with the mind, the combination assumed a probability so nearly zero as to render the occurrence nothing short of miraculous.

In spite of the difficulties Georgiana was facing, he was greatly reassured by how she spoke of them; surely she could not write about them so intelligently and reasonably without having in some measure gained mastery over them. He went over those paragraphs several times to be sure he had taken their meaning completely, and was satisfied.

When she then passed on to Miss Elizabeth Bennet, however, and her comments showed such depth of perception that he had to stop yet again, and ask himself just how much of his deeper thoughts he had revealed, for she seemed all too aware of how much he had found to value in Miss Elizabeth Bennet. In addition, she expressed a wish to meet her, and a desire to hear more of her in his next correspondence. Great Heavens, he thought, first Miss Bingley and now Georgiana: are all women gifted with second sight where matters of the heart are concerned? No man in the world would have read into his letters what Georgiana seemed to have discovered; he would wager any sum that Bingley was entirely ignorant of the fact that he had ever looked twice at Miss Elizabeth Bennet.

On one point Georgiana seemed less acute: in spite of his descriptions of Mrs. Bennet, Georgiana declared herself at a loss to understand his objections to the connection. He knew Georgiana to be cognizant of the importance of good breeding—not only had this been one of the basic tenets of her upbringing and their family status, but, more practically, animal husbandry was every where a concern in Derbyshire, and not a month went by when the results of a breeding trial, or plans for another, were not discussed in her hearing. That she could miss so obvious an association between one generation and the next surprised him. He must, while he was in London, find some books to help enlighten her on this point. Malthus...no. Locke, Hume...no. —No: the Comte de Buffon was the very man....

While he waited for the others, he took the opportunity to write his reply to Georgiana, and had sealed it and handed it to Perkins before any one else appeared. He gave himself back to the quiet of the morning; the windows of the salon, facing east, showed a crisp, clear day, with the last wisps of mist just burning away from about the feet of the deep woods that lay in that direction; he sat, musing on various matters, as the remainder of a quiet country morning unfolded.

"'Morning, Darcy!" Bingley's voice brought him back to himself. "Lovely morning!" Darcy put away Georgiana's letters and agreed: "It is indeed. It would be a fine opportunity for a ride, once you have broken your fast."

Bingley stepped happily over to the sideboard with expectant pleasure. "An excellent thought!" cried he. He casually added, "I was toying with the idea of wandering over to Longbourn; just to be sure Miss Bennet is quite well." He began helping himself to a large portion of muffins and savoury sausages, with an Olympian dollop of jam to go with them. Darcy shook his head in horror at the thought of such a breakfast, and took several sips of black coffee to clear the imagined taste from his palate.

Agreeing to his friend's suggestion, however, he said, "That would be a pleasant little ride. If we come back through the fields we might give the horses a bit of exercise." He privately thought that it might be as well to test his resolve concerning Miss Elizabeth Bennet, and that this would offer a fine opportunity to do so.

Two hours later, after Bingley's breakfast and a change of clothes, they accordingly set off for Meryton. Bingley was

Chapter XVII

sharply dressed indeed, and Darcy hardly less so. Perkins had heard their destination without comment, but had been more thoughtfully absorbed than usual as he handed various articles of clothing to his master. The result, Darcy thought as he had viewed himself in the mirror, was quite acceptable; he lifted his chest unconsciously as Perkins put the finishing flourishes on his neck cloth.

During the ride to the village, Bingley chattered happily on about inconsequential matters; Darcy was content to listen in silence. The air was still and the sun bright, and the only sounds were the birds and a distant woodsman's axe making a muted counterpoint to their horses' hooves. The crisp air, with an occasional whiff of sharp wood-smoke to accent the damp odour of leaf mould, sharpened his mind and refreshed his body. They reached Meryton after a leisurely quarter-hour's ride. As they rounded the corner into the square, Bingley peered ahead and said, "Darcy, is not that the Bennet ladies across the way?"

And so it was. Almost all of the Bennet sisters were gathered in a congenial knot with several gentlemen on the other side of the square. The gentlemen from Netherfield rode across to them as Bingley called out: "Miss Bennet — good morning! We were just riding to Longbourn to ask after your health, and here you are. What luck!"

Miss Bennet curtsied to them both, and Darcy bowed from the saddle in acknowledgement. Standing along with the Bennet girls there was a parson, unknown to Darcy, and one of the officers of Colonel Forster's militia, whose name, Darcy recalled, was Mr. Denny. Miss Elizabeth Bennet stood off to one side with a gentleman whose back was to him; schooling himself not to allow his gaze to rest too long on her, he allowed it to travel to the gentleman. At that moment the man turned, and...Wickham! It was as though a gun had fired at him from point-blank range: he felt the blood surge in his veins, his vision narrowed until he could see nothing but his enemy, and he was suddenly deaf to every thing around him. Profound and riotous feelings — a fierce anger, dark and irresistible, older than justice —

Into Hertfordshire

coursed through him in an instant, leaving him absolutely still in its wake, poised, as to strike. His mind cast about hastily for some means of crushing the hateful, evil creature before him, but there were too many people, too many witnesses. Within him a desperate urge to violence did battle with rational self-preservation. At his side, Bingley continued to rattle away, unaware of Darcy's private struggles.

Darcy had no notion of how long the two of them held their positions thus, but at length Wickham raised a hand, late and reluctant, to his hat; to Darcy this was beyond every thing—acknowledge this creature? He gave the least of nods, giving his reviled *bête noir* to know that he had been seen, and had best look about him in future. With a long, baleful look into the eyes of his foe, he turned his horse away. He rode off, neither knowing nor caring if Bingley followed. He maintained his rigid self-command with difficulty; the effort was akin to walking down a flight of stairs holding two very full glasses of wine: every motion an exercise of will and concentration of the highest degree. He must not allow any unconstrained movement, for fear that any slightest loss of self-control would escalate into an uncontainable, irrepressibly violent rage. Wickham, here in Meryton....Wickham, standing right next to Elizabeth.... Dear God above...he hardly knew how to imagine worse. Was this possible? Was this real? His mind worked feverishly, trying to comprehend this sudden appearance of the greatest evil of his life—in this place, and at this time.

He was nearly out of the square when he finally realised that Bingley was riding next to him, speaking urgently. He turned blankly towards him and eventually brought his features into focus. Bingley stared at him, concern etched in every line of his face. "Darcy, what is it?" he demanded. "What has happened? Are you unwell? Stop, man, and tell me what I can do!"

"I am well," said Darcy in a broken voice. "It is...I am not...there is nothing wrong...that is, I am not ill. I will be well in a moment." With the return of speech, his mind

Chapter XVII

seemed to become his own again. He drew a deep breath and looked about, re-establishing himself in the world.

"Dear God, Darcy, you gave me a turn! What on Earth has happened to you?"

Darcy reached out and leaned his hand reassuringly on Bingley's shoulder for a moment, but made no immediate answer. They rode on some little distance before he could reply. "That man: have I ever mentioned that name to you?"

"Mr. Wickham? Not that I recall. Are you acquainted with him?"

"Yes, but I try not to speak his name, if I can avoid it. He...I have...." He breathed in deeply. "Perhaps you remember my once having spoken of people who are nothing but a stain on our land: he is just such a one. He is in every way unworthy to draw breath, yet he roams England freely and unhindered. How is that right? How is that just? God help me—what is he doing *here*?"

"Great Heavens, Darcy—what has he done?"

This gave Darcy pause: he must not blurt out too much in his present state; no one outside himself and his cousin Edmund knew of Georgiana's intended elopement last summer, and he was particularly anxious that Georgiana's character be preserved where Bingley was concerned. He said cautiously, "I can tell you some things, the least of his transgressions, but the rest involves others and I must hold what I know in confidence."

"Tell me what you can, then."

Darcy deliberated within himself as they rode on. At length he replied: "Very well; but, Bingley, I would have this go no farther. Please tell your sisters only that an antipathy exists between us from prior injuries—that will suffice." Bingley nodded his agreement and Darcy went on: "All my life he has been an evil to me; he grew up on our estate. His father was Pemberley's steward under my father. He was a very worthy man, a very skilful man, and my father was grateful to him for his service. My father therefore became the younger man's godfather, and liked

Into Hertfordshire

him exceedingly well—for, as we know, the Devil can play a very charming rôle if He chooses. My father was therefore most liberal in supporting and advancing him. He hoped to see him enter the Church—imagine it, the Church! —and had left it with me to give him the best living on the estate, should he wish it. I, on the other hand, had seen him grow from petty thieving in the pantry to outright larceny and worse, but always careful, so careful, to disguise it from my father. And lies—good God, Bingley, the lies he told! I tried for years to open my father's eyes to them, but Wickham always found a way to win him over, while I was left to look the villain myself, for always picking on a younger man, less well-off than myself. After a while I stopped trying; it only cost me my father's esteem without correcting the fault, or even urging my father to caution.

"After his father's death and that of my own, the fellow spurned the living that my father had intended for him, and applied to me for more immediate remuneration in its stead. I was greatly relieved, as I knew well enough that he must never become a clergyman. He spoke of studying law; that seemed appropriate, I thought: let the Devil take care of His own. I therefore sent him three thousand pounds—and, mind you, that was in *addition* to the thousand my father left him in his will."

"Most generous," murmured Bingley.

"I thought so, too, and felt it all the more so when he cleared out of Derbyshire leaving several hundreds of debt behind him, which I was obliged to discharge," said Darcy with some heat. "But I wished, out of respect for my father's memory, to honour his intention of securing the man in some profession. I suppose I knew he would never make a serious study of it, but when he said he wished to read law I took him at his word. To tell the truth, I was only too glad to pay him off and be done with him. From time to time I heard rumours of a very dissipated lifestyle; drinking, gaming, wenching—the full extent of sins open to a man—but, as I had washed my hands of him, I paid little attention.

Chapter XVII

Then, a little over a year ago, he came back at me for the preferment of the living."

"What!"

"Just so. And again, these are the *least* of his transgressions, as I know them. He had managed to consume four thousands in less than five years, in a life of the foulest pursuits imaginable, and now had the effrontery to represent to me that he wished to take orders and become the quiet country clergyman. You may imagine my reply to this entreaty."

"As if you could give over the care of Pemberley's dependents to such a man!"

"Indeed. But I underestimated him; during the course of this last year he sought his revenge by making a very serious effort to embroil the Darcy name in a shockingly dishonourable affair. I cannot say the particulars, save that it was foiled only by a most fortunate turn of luck. It would have made him rich, but it would have brought disgrace upon us that generations could not expunge."

"Good Lord! The blackguard! After all your family had done for him! But how could he have managed such a thing?"

"Through his lies. I tell you, Bingley, he is mendacity itself; he will lie even when the truth would serve. I have never encountered another creature that could come within miles of him for the depth and breadth of his lies. And in telling them, he has the air of a saint; the more incredible the tale, the more compellingly he tells it. For most people, my father included, the very fact that his claims are so nearly incredible ensures belief: the sheer audacity of his lies makes it seem impossible that they could be other than the absolute truth."

"Was he always like this?" Bingley wished to know.

"That is what strains my understanding to the limit, Bingley, challenges every thing I would wish to believe about my fellow man: for yes, he *was* always thus. Before he knew care, before he knew want—I do believe he was this way from the cradle. There is nothing in his history to excuse him. That an animal such as he, parading about disguised as a man, can pass for a civilised being, casts into doubt all I have believed about virtue's necessary and inevitable triumph over evil."

"Why did you not have him taken in charge?"

"There is another example of his unqualified malevolence; in so doing I should have had to expose innocent people to misconstructions of the most damaging nature. He planned it all so that he took no appreciable risks himself, using others' reputations as his shield."

They rode on for some distance. Bingley broke their silence: "But, come, Darcy; we know that Evil does walk abroad to-day, as it ever has. We must not allow it to gain ascendancy over us. Surely it is our part, our duty, to stand up to it and move on." Darcy looked seriously at his friend and nodded solemnly without speaking. He did not say that he had been trying to stand up to this particular evil all his life, and had failed on every occasion.

Chapter Eighteen

*D*arcy spent the rest of the day in his chambers. Those who consistently deny their emotions are ill-prepared to deal with them when once they have broken free, and his encounter with Wickham had shaken him deeply; he felt unequal to company, but neither could he find ease in solitude. His one comfort was that, with Wickham here, Georgiana must be safe from him. Not that he could imagine that she was in any danger from her feelings for him, not at this late date, but it had occurred to him early on that Wickham might attempt to blackmail her on the strength of their planned elopement. He had, of course, left instructions of the most exigent nature that Wickham never be allowed on his lands again, but Wickham was resourceful; there was no telling what allies he might have still in Pemberley. He took out her last letter, and found some comfort in his turn by the improvement he observed there; it did not occur to him to realise that their rôles were now reversed: that she was now become the source of solace in *his* need.

Darcy awoke the next day still disturbed in his mind, and spent the better part of it brooding before the fire in his own chambers; the weather was cold and he did not wish to ride, and he still felt unfit for company. He had Perkins convey his apologies to his friends. He tried on various occasions to divert himself with a book, but could last no more than a few pages before casting it aside in frustration. He thought back over his long association with Wickham, trying yet again to find some explanation, some *raison d'être,* that might excuse such a being's existence. As a philosopher and man of reason he felt compelled to seek such an excuse; it was not possible that God and Nature could suffer to exist a creature so wholly negative in character; there must be *something* to justify his life, and also, perhaps, a reason why he should have been sent to burden Darcy's. But he was, he had to admit to himself, too prejudiced to think dispassionately on the subject; Wickham had too often and too easily emerged victorious over him, in his attempts to dislodge him from that place in his father's regard which he so little deserved, for Darcy to be able to set aside his temper and consider the problem rationally.

Darcy was also deeply disturbed by his loss of decorum on Tuesday's meeting. To have his anger on display for Miss Elizabeth Bennet, and, indeed, the entire village to see, and to know how Wickham revelled in being able to goad him into a loss of self-possession, mortified and angered him by turns. The frustrations and doubts he had felt as a young man—seeing his father taken in, yet powerless to convince him of Wickham's faults—came back again and again to plague his thoughts; he feared to see that same patient yet disappointed look in Elizabeth's eyes. Only the perusal of his sister's letter brought him any peace, and he turned to it repeatedly through the many sombre hours of the day.

On Thursday morning he felt himself sufficiently recovered, and, indeed, obliged by the demands of merest civility, to venture downstairs to breakfast. He was the first down, as usual, but he soon was joined by his friend and Miss Bingley; the Hursts rarely appeared before the rest had finished their breakfast and set out on the day's activities. Bingley treated him with kind forbearance, and must have given his sister some idea of what had occurred, as she was more solicitous than ever to his needs.

The two of them, he soon found, were setting out early that morning to personally deliver a number of invitations to the ball. The bulk of the invitations were to go out in the morning post, but issuing invitations to the more prominent members of local society was to be performed in person. On this occasion, in contrast to certain other occasions in the past, Darcy was minded to approve the simple enthusiasms and open, heartfelt cordiality of his friend; his uncomplicat-

Chapter XVIII

ed goodness shone like a beacon against the malignant duplicity of Wickham.

After they had taken themselves off, Darcy indulged himself in another cup of coffee, shaking off the last residue of emotion from his two days' sober introspection. The morning post arrived while he was still at table, and in it he was pleased to find another letter from his sister; he turned to it with a welcome sense of relief. She had written it on the prior Sunday, and it dealt with his observations on Miss Bingley and her jealousy towards Miss Elizabeth Bennet; he found great interest in what she had to say about Miss Bingley. Her description of her matrimonial intentions and outlook, her desire to make a "conquest" and her "pragmatic" view of men, sent a shock of amazement into him, and he suddenly felt that he had been altogether unaware of how dangerously close to the precipice he had been so carelessly wandering. He was astounded that his sister could harbour such knowledge, and exceedingly gratified by her sound advice. He determined to redouble his vigilance in future.

His coffee finished, he drifted into the library with the idea of finding something to read; the relief of thinking about something other than Wickham had given him a renewed sense of purpose, and a need of intellectual exercise. While he was going over the shelves, which, while nothing to Pemberley's collection, held certain volumes that his did not—including some early editions of Rabelais' work, with some very lively woodcuts—he was alarmed by the arrival of a footman to deliver an express from Pemberley. Darcy tore it open the moment the door was closed, fearful that some ill had befallen Georgiana—Wickham was first in his thoughts—but the letter's opening sentence gave him relief. The second, however, confused him: that Georgiana should write him express about a ball was singular in the extreme. Whatever was she thinking?

On reading the entire letter, however, he became more troubled than confused. Her earnestly expressed desire, that he should stay to the ball and dance with Miss Elizabeth

Into Hertfordshire

Bennet, tugged at his own wishes. He had thought, on more than one occasion, what pleasure it would give him to take Elizabeth's hand for a set, and more recently had prided himself on his willing sacrifice of that pleasure for her sake. But now Georgiana was most solemnly entreating him to abandon that position for *her* sake; whose interests were to take precedence? At first his inclinations followed his wishes, and he felt that he might stay to take her hand at Bingley's ball. But, when he delved more deeply into the matter, he had to ask himself, not who would benefit by such a scheme, but who would suffer the more. His sister's wishes were, he felt, ill-formed and not well founded, while his decision not to distinguish Miss Elizabeth Bennet was founded on the secure tenets of probity and honour. To raise any expectation in her would violate both; therefore the wisest and best course remained the same: he must not show her any particular regard. Georgiana would understand, he assured himself, when he explained it to her fully. In the next moment, however, he reminded himself of the solemn promise he had given her, and which she had invoked, to do anything in his power to improve her spirits. How was such a conflict to be resolved?

He returned to the shelves of books, still troubled in his mind with the many particulars of the past several days; he settled at last on Montaigne's *Essais*, but, after trying one or two different essays, he found the ambiguity of the author's too-human tolerance of man's foibles did not suit his need for clarity at the moment; he hesitated over Hume's *Treatise*, but that author's view that reason was subservient to one's passions seemed too much a defence for Wickham. He therefore went back to the Renaissance for More's *Utopia*; the simplicity and harmony More had imagined was what he wanted to soothe his sensibilities. He rang for another coffee, and settled himself into a deep chair with his book.

He passed an hour or two in this pursuit, occasionally lifting his thoughts back to the issue of the ball, but to little

Chapter XVIII

effect. He was still thus engaged when Bingley appeared in search of him. "Darcy?" his voice sounded at the door.

"Bingley! Welcome back. Have you secured a grand attendance for your ball?"

But, entering, his friend had no smiles for him on this occasion. "Darcy, I have something to tell you," said he, his manner subdued.

"What is it, Bingley? Is all well?"

"I cannot tell. I...I saw that fellow, the one you... Darcy, he has joined the regiment. He is one of Forster's officers. I saw him after I delivered the invitation to Colonel Forster."

"He will stay on in Meryton, then." said Darcy.

"He will. And, I say, Darcy, I issued a general invitation to all the officers, not knowing.... He will be at the ball." Bingley peered anxiously at his friend. "I did not know what best I should do. I had already spoken to Colonel Forster; would you have me exclude him from the invitation?"

Darcy hesitated, his desire to injure Wickham at odds with his need to protect his sister's character. With a grimace of distaste he answered, "No. Colonel Forster could hardly pass over such an exclusion without enquiry as to the reason, and I can give none of substance without naming those innocents I mentioned. And, as you have said, we must stand up to Evil, not run from it. No, I can face him down, if it comes to that, but I doubt it will; he is, for all his audacity, a coward at heart. He will avoid my presence; he will not attend, knowing that I should be there." He spoke with more confidence than he felt; looking at Bingley with a wry expression he added, "If, however, I am mistaken on this point, I shall look to you, my friend, to help keep my neck out of the gallows' noose, and be so good as to remove any weapons that might be lying about." He spoke lightly, but a harsh and earnest truth could be felt behind his words.

"As you would have it, Darcy," Bingley assured him sincerely. "Only tell me if you change your mind."

Into Hertfordshire

Darcy nodded absently, and Bingley, after a serious look at his friend, quit the room. Wickham in the village for the winter — this put things in a very different light; he could not leave Netherfield until Elizabeth had been put on her guard; the injury Wickham could do her far outweighed that which he might do, in requesting her hand for a dance. The image of Wickham standing at her side leapt up before him, and he felt all the danger to her of Wickham's continued residence in such proximity; they could not help but be thrown in each other's way. But, when he considered how such a communication was to be accomplished, he was perplexed. The same objection to informing Colonel Forster must also apply here; he did not see how he might convince Elizabeth of Wickham's true character without compromising Georgiana. Elizabeth would not, could not, listen to such a representation without demanding to know his authority, and this he could not give; and to attempt to put her on her guard without the necessary details might have entirely the opposite effect: such a seemingly unwarranted attack might serve to raise her interest in Wickham, rather than diminish it, as it had done with his father.

He considered giving her the bare facts of the case without names, and merely asking her to trust him for its veracity; but then he reminded himself that this was Wickham he was dealing with; he knew from years of experience that Wickham's lies sounded better than his truths — even to his own father. Unless he wished to stay there at Netherfield all winter to counteract Wickham's lies, he must do better than this. His options appeared to be rather limited. The full truth, and ask for her secrecy? Unthinkable. If it once got loose within her family, her mother and younger sisters would have it spread from Dover to Derby inside three days. No, he told himself, there must be a better way; of what use was the intellect, if not for just such a problem as this? He must somehow protect both Georgiana and Elizabeth; the ball was on Tuesday: five days and a half to find the answer. He looked around him at works representing the collected wisdom of the ages, stacked in sedate and

Chapter XVIII

stately rows around the walls of Bingley's library, and was confident of success.

Chapter Nineteen

*B*y Tuesday morning, Darcy's confidence had eroded into despair; the problem was intractable. Without giving up his sister's secret, there could be no exposing Wickham; without such exposure, there could be no safeguarding Elizabeth. And since he would never subject his sister to society's contempt, nor himself to its condemnation for making public her private affairs, there was an end to it.

He was at times uncertain whether he ought even to attend the ball—he did not think he could stand by and watch Elizabeth on Wickham's arm. But neither would he allow himself to run from Wickham's presence—rather would he take her hand for every dance, if it came to that. He could only hope that there might arise an opportunity for him to make such communication as would give her some degree of warning, some measure of protection against Wickham's deceits. Failing to arrive at a more definite solution, he determined that that was the only course open to him: he must take her hand, and trust to luck to supply the needed opportunity.

After dinner Perkins had laid out only one set of clothes for the evening: his finest. The linen would have put newly fallen snow to shame, and Darcy could have shaved in the reflection given off by his shoes. Darcy dressed with something of the air of a knight donning his armour prior to battle; if he was to face Wickham, he would do so with every advantage at his disposal. He reassured himself that, if nothing else, his attire for the evening must represent six months' income to Wickham, and a lieutenant's regimentals could not hold a candle to the exquisitely tailored coat and breeches Perkins so carefully draped on his form.

Darcy was downstairs in very good time in hopes of finding Miss Elizabeth Bennet alone before Wickham

Chapter XIX

should arrive; he therefore positioned himself to one side of the stairs to watch the arrivals. The Lucas family was first to arrive, led by Sir William, who bowed so often and so indiscriminately that Darcy actually saw him bow to a startled footman—who nonetheless returned the bow with perfect aplomb. Darcy ensconced himself well behind the banister, hoping to postpone the enjoyment of receiving Sir William's effusive courtesies. Bingley was smiling brightly at every one as they entered, while Miss Bingley maintained a decidedly more formal and proper civility, as if she wished to atone for her brother's lack of reserve. After perhaps a quarter-hour dawdling thus amongst the potted plants, the arrival of the Bennets, heralded by the mother's shrill voice from the drive, rewarded Darcy with the sight of Elizabeth he had been waiting for. She was very much in looks; her eyes were bright and a look of happy anticipation played about her features as she took in the scene, making signs of recognition to her friends and neighbours. Darcy felt as though he had never been seeing her before with proper appreciation of her beauty; she was without question the loveliest woman he knew: her eyes and smile were perfection, and the gown she wore this evening set off her figure to such a degree Darcy had difficulty taking his eyes away from her. His determination to protect her from Wickham was strengthened by the apprehension of such a flawless woman being sullied by the attentions of so low a creature. His eyes followed Elizabeth as she drifted with the rest of her family down the reception line and into the drawing-room, where the bulk of those already present were raising a clamour of greetings, laughter, and the communal noises of the occasion. He allowed the crush at the door to subside, then passed into the drawing-room himself.

Elizabeth, as Darcy entered the room, was standing with her youngest sister and an officer, Mr. Denny—he who had stood with Wickham in the street at Meryton. Unable to hear what was said, Darcy nonetheless observed that Elizabeth appeared disconcerted by his words, and even somewhat cast down. Her shoulders drooped slightly, and the smile fled from her face. Moved by seeing her thus discomfited, when they parted he approached to make his greeting, hoping to divert her thoughts or perhaps even to assuage her feelings, whatever might be called for in the case. He stepped around to face her and bowed.

"Miss Elizabeth Bennet; good evening. It is a great pleasure to see you again. You are well, I trust?"

She seemed almost startled to see him, but this Darcy attributed to her discomposure, for, looking over his shoulder, she answered shortly: "Perfectly well, I thank you, Sir. Will you excuse me, please?" And with a preoccupied air, she stepped around him and crossed the room to where her friend, Miss Charlotte Lucas, stood against the wall. Concerned, hoping Elizabeth was not unwell, he watched them both for a time. That she was distressed was evident, but the case seemed to need only sympathy, for, after a few minutes of speech from her and consoling looks from her friend, Elizabeth's good humour revived. She began to smile and laugh again, and was soon entertaining Miss Lucas, as well; she, too, began to laugh behind her fan at what Darcy was sure must have been some of Elizabeth's intentionally outlandish opinions. Satisfied, he turned away; a breath he had not known he was holding became a sigh of relief: all was well—the evening could proceed according to plan. He began to think of moving towards her again through the crowd.

At that moment he felt a touch at his sleeve and turned to find Miss Bingley; said she: "I hope you will forgive me, Mr. Darcy, but I fear I am committed to Colonel Forster to open the ball. You will not mind, I trust?"

Darcy locked his features into neutrality and said with a bow, "Not at all, Miss Bingley; quite proper."

"I do not know when I shall be free from my duties as hostess…" she paused, waiting for Darcy to take the hint.

"I am quite sure we shall find ample time to surfeit ourselves with dancing during the evening, Miss Bingley," was Darcy's careful response. On his side, he was already

Chapter XIX

surfeited with dancing, if it meant partnering her. His reply satisfied Miss Bingley, however, and she turned away to attend to her other guests. Darcy again breathed his relief and looked for Elizabeth; she still chatted with Miss Lucas, and as none of the other gentlemen present had approached them, Darcy felt some assurance that no one had engaged her yet.

Bingley briefly broke away from his other guests then, to approach his friend with this news: "Well, Darcy, you were right—that fellow has stayed away. I have just had it from Colonel Forster, who tendered his regrets to me. He has gone to Town."

This intelligence brought considerable relief to Darcy's mind. While he had been nearly certain Wickham would not attend, he could not but have moments of doubt, and Bingley's information was welcome, indeed. In addition, Wickham would have no opportunity to influence Elizabeth with his lies if he were absent; moreover, as it had rained steadily most of the week, he could have had little occasion to be in company with her prior to this evening. Encouraged, he nodded his thanks to his friend and again began moving across the room to Elizabeth.

That intention was forestalled, however; just then the musicians struck up their instruments, and Elizabeth was approached by a parson who appeared to have made a prior claim; bowing like the veriest dandy, he took her hand with excessively studied manners and led her to the floor. Darcy was disappointed and a little alarmed, as the man was the same one he had seen in the square with Wickham and the others. Not knowing anything about him other than the fact that he had seen him with Wickham, he was concerned lest the man was in some way connected with him. His alarm was quieted, however, by the fact that Elizabeth gave Miss Lucas a droll look of martyred anguish behind the parson's back as he turned to lead her to the floor. Darcy smiled and relaxed: this might hold some amusement.

In truth, it went a little beyond amusing, for the man was an absolutely wretched dancer; that, coupled with his

Into Hertfordshire

odd and affected mannerisms, made him, and his poor partner, an object in front of the whole room. Darcy believed that he spent more time bowing and apologising to those whose dance he interrupted with his missteps, than he did leading Elizabeth through the set. To Darcy, incompetence in any activity was deplorable; as little as he liked the pastime, he had made it his business to be able to perform it with acceptable skill. Elizabeth bore with her partner as well as any one could, but it was clear to every one in the room how she must be suffering; to make matters worse, he kept her hand for a second dance. Darcy pitied her, but he reflected that this would at least make him a more desirable alternative.

Just as the set was ending, and Darcy was beginning once again to move in Elizabeth's direction, he spied Miss Bingley enter the room and look about as though seeking some one; he was instantly persuaded that he was her quarry. He quickly ducked behind a conveniently placed screen. She surveyed the room in one quick revolution, going up on her toes to see over the heads of the couples returning to their seats; she then left by the same door through which she had entered. Darcy emerged cautiously from his hiding place, only to see Elizabeth be claimed for the next dance by an officer, one whom he recognised from his dinner at the mess, but whose name he did not know. Cursing his luck, with a bit left over for Miss Bingley, he waited out the dance while keeping a weather-eye out for the redcoats, the parson, Miss Bingley, or any one else who might prevent his asking Elizabeth's hand for the following set.

When that dance was over and Elizabeth was released by the officer, she crossed to the side of the room away from Darcy, where her friend Miss Lucas still stood watching the couples on the dance floor. He moved with celerity to seize his chance: she had her back to him as he approached, but, on seeing Miss Lucas curtsey, she turned to face him. Without hesitation he hurriedly said, "Miss Elizabeth Bennet: would you do me the honour of dancing the next with me?"

"I...I...yes, I will, Sir."

Chapter XIX

His petition had clearly taken her by surprise, and he grimaced inwardly at the awkward manner in which he had made it; yet, she had accepted him, and he was satisfied. He bowed his thanks and retreated, gratified to have finally achieved his object, his mind already on the problem of how best to broach the subject of Wickham. When the dance began again, he still had yet to make up his mind. But on taking Elizabeth's hand and leading her to the floor in his turn, he was suddenly struck—he held her hand in his, and she was to dance with him. A kind of warmth, unlike any he had ever felt, suffused him: thrilling, yet strangely comforting at the same time; he gazed at his partner for a long moment, amazed at the pleasing distinction to which he was arrived in being able at last to stand opposite such a woman. He was even able to accept with tolerably good grace the looks he and his partner garnered from about the room. The warmth continued within him as they entered the set, and he was content to move through the first forms of the dance in silence, savouring the pleasure of the moment and the sensation of her hand in his.

After some little time, his partner spoke: "This dance is a favourite of mine."

The dance was the minuet, which had long been Darcy's favourite, too. He appreciated its grace, and its stately and mathematical progression. Gratified by the concurrence of their taste, he agreed: "And mine. The orchestra is very fine, as well."

Elizabeth made no reply and Darcy allowed his thoughts to drift back again into his reverie. It lasted some minutes more, until she broke into his thoughts, saying: 'It is *your* turn to say something now, Mr. Darcy. *I* talked about the dance, and *you* ought to make some kind of remark on the size of the room, or the number of couples."

Darcy hastily brought himself to the present, embarrassed by his lapse. This was the Elizabeth he so enjoyed: witty, confident, and yet so consistently gracious and charming in manner. It was wonderful how she could manage to take him to task and utterly enchant him in the same breath. He smiled at her, saying, "I shall be happy to comply, I assure you; you have but to hint at what you wish said, and it shall be so."

"Very well. That reply will do for the present. Perhaps by and by I may observe that private balls are much pleasanter than public ones. —But *now* we may be silent."

By which, given her habitual contrariety of speech, Darcy concluded that she wished him to continue speaking. Darcy had been thoroughly versed in etiquette, and knew that the thing to do when you have nothing of substance to offer, is to ask a question. He therefore re-joined, "Do you talk by rule, then, while you are dancing?"

"Sometimes. One must speak a little, you know. It would look odd to be entirely silent for half an hour together; and yet for the advantage of some, conversation ought to be so arranged, as that they may have the trouble of saying as little as possible."

Delighted by this playful attack on what good manners must comprise, he said, "Are you consulting your own feelings in the present case, or do you imagine that you are gratifying mine?" Mindful of his reputation for reserve, he rather hoped he might hear her deny the latter part of his question in a manner favourable to his character.

"Both," replied Elizabeth, "for I have always seen a great similarity in the turn of our minds. —We are each of an unsocial, taciturn disposition, unwilling to speak, unless we expect to say something that will amaze the whole room, and be handed down to posterity with all the éclat of a proverb."

Now she *was* teasing him. "This is no very striking resemblance of your own character, I am sure," said he, with a smile. "How near it may be to *mine*, I cannot pretend to say. —*You* think it a faithful portrait undoubtedly." He tried again to gently probe about her opinion of himself.

"I must not decide on my own performance," she deflected his enquiry. Her manner throughout, however, had been playful, and Darcy was in no doubt that this exercise of her charms was entirely for his benefit.

Chapter XIX

A short silence followed, and Darcy felt it incumbent on him to start the next subject. It had often occurred to him that his youth in Derbyshire must have had many similarities with Elizabeth's in Hertfordshire, as Country life was much the same no matter where one was raised. As a boy he had always looked forward to a walk into Lambton, the little town that was to Pemberley as Meryton was to Longbourn, and, with this in view, he asked, "Do not you and your sisters very often walk to Meryton?"

Her reply was not at all what he had anticipated. "Indeed, we do. When you met us there the other day, we had just been forming a new acquaintance."

Wickham! The warmth within him vanished like the light of a candle blown out. He paused for a moment to adjust his thoughts; here then, was the opportunity he had been waiting for—although now that it had come, he wished it had not. Choosing his words carefully, so as not to expose too much ill-will, he made his attempt: "Mr. Wickham is blessed with such happy manners as may ensure his *making* friends—whether he may be equally capable of *retaining* them, is less certain." He paused to see how she might respond.

He had not long to wait. "He has been so unlucky as to lose *your* friendship," Elizabeth retorted in an accusatory tone, "and in a manner which he is likely to suffer from all his life."

With astonishment did Darcy realise that Wickham had somehow already reached Elizabeth with his lies. He hardly knew what to say; clearly Wickham had fed her some tale that put Darcy in a bad light, but, even if he knew what Wickham had said, the middle of a ball-room was hardly the place to defend himself. Yet he must somehow make her see the truth about Wickham. Still, he was painfully aware that he had ever been weak in persuasion; it was in reasoned discourse and logic that his strengths lay. What could he say that might convince her? He found himself trapped within the same doubts and tangled thoughts that had plagued him since the Thursday prior.

Into Hertfordshire

Before he could adjust his thoughts and render them into some form of speech, Sir William Lucas made as if to pass them; but, stopping, he offered them a compliment on how well they looked dancing together. Darcy, trying yet again to adjust his thoughts, was struggling to find words to reply when Sir William went on to say, "I must hope to have this pleasure often repeated, especially when a certain desirable event, my dear Miss Eliza, shall take place," and with this he bent a significant glance in the direction of Miss Bennet and Bingley, who were standing out of the dance behind Darcy and his partner. "What congratulations will then flow in! I appeal to Mr. Darcy—but let me not interrupt you, Sir. You will not thank me for detaining you from the bewitching converse of that young lady, whose bright eyes are also upbraiding me." He beamed kindly at them and turned away.

Darcy met this news regarding his friend with irritation; at every turn this evening, some one was waiting to step between him and his wishes. Now what was Bingley about? Forcing down the anger and frustration that, he knew, would render him unable to think clearly, he turned his attention to Bingley. He could see he was deep in conversation with Elizabeth's eldest sister: so deep, indeed, that he was unaware of several people who were standing near him, obviously waiting to speak with him. Just then he took Miss Bennet's hand, and, without so much as a glance at his other guests, led her out into the dance. Several of those waiting shared tolerant smiles at this, together with a knowing shake of the head. Darcy had never before seen his friend so enraptured by a woman as to fail in civility to others—and at his own ball! Only a true attachment could explain, or excuse, such behaviour.

He turned back to his partner and found that she, too, was watching the couple with interest. What with the consternation caused by this new intelligence and his anxious desire to warn her about Wickham, it took several moments before he could arrange his thoughts sufficiently to take up the conversation again. He had lost the train of their last

Chapter XIX

subject, and turning back to her, he apologised: "Sir William's interruption has made me forget what we were talking of."

"I do not think we were speaking at all," answered Elizabeth. She seemed out of humour as she said, "Sir William could not have interrupted any two people in the room who had less to say for themselves. We have tried two or three subjects already without success, and what we are to talk of next I cannot imagine."

"What think you of books?" Darcy ventured, knowing how devoted she was to reading. He kept his tone studiously light, and he smiled as he spoke, for he heartily wished to change the tenor of the conversation to a more congenial one. He hoped gradually to be able to bring their discussion back around to the subject of Wickham in a way more conducive to the communication he had in view. But the lady was not inclined to cooperate.

"Books—oh! no," said she. "I am sure we never read the same, or not with the same feelings."

He failed to understand why she should object to the topic, and observed: "I am sorry you think so; but if that be the case, there can at least be no want of subject. We may compare our different opinions."

"No—I cannot talk of books in a ball-room; my head is always full of something else."

She had a distracted air as she spoke, leaving him in doubt of her true thoughts. He asked uncertainly, "The *present* always occupies you in such scenes—does it?"

"Yes, always," she answered absently. Darcy was at a loss as to what might next be said, as his partner's mind was clearly elsewhere. She suddenly took his eye with hers, saying, "I remember hearing you once say, Mr. Darcy, that you hardly ever forgave—that your resentment once created was unappeasable. You are very cautious, I suppose, as to its *being created*."

Surprised at this sudden change of topic, he nevertheless declared confidently, "I am."

"And never allow yourself to be blinded by prejudice?"

"I hope not."

"It is particularly incumbent on those who never change their opinion, to be secure of judging properly at first."

He was confused by these questions and her sober manner; was she thinking of Wickham, or Bingley, or something else entirely? —"May I ask to what these questions tend?"

She pursed her lips and frowned, looking as though she were trying to clear her thoughts. "Merely to the illustration of *your* character. I am trying to make it out."

"And what is your success?" That she should make such an attempt was pleasing, but the substance of their exchange up to that point was such that he was uncertain that he should be equally well pleased with the result.

"I do not get on at all," she replied, with a shake of her head. "I hear such different accounts of you as puzzle me exceedingly."

Here was the illumination he sought; her manner as she spoke and looked at him convinced him: he was quite sure he knew the source of those "different accounts"—he wished that he could know what manner of lies Wickham might have given her. "I can readily believe," he said, trying with all the sincerity at his command to make her understand the gravity of his words, "that reports may vary greatly with respect to me; and I could wish, Miss Bennet, that you were not to sketch my character at the present moment, as there is reason to fear that the performance would reflect no credit on either."

"But if I do not take your likeness now, I may never have another opportunity," she declared. Her manner was not contentious, but neither was it accommodating.

Darcy's irritation and frustration, which had been struggling to break free almost since he had first approached to offer her his compliments, and fuelled by all the times he had found himself thwarted by Wickham

Chapter XIX

throughout his youth, flashed into anger: she *would* not oblige him; she *would* not understand; she had rather believe Wickham, a man of no standing whom she had known only a week! As had always been the case with his father where Wickham was concerned, his words had fallen on deaf ears. Controlling himself with difficulty, he replied, "I would by no means suspend any pleasure of yours," and bit down to hold back the heated words that wanted to follow. They proceeded down the dance, each one holding their own counsel; on his side, however, his anger was soon replaced by remorse, as he realised that the trouble lay not with her, but with Wickham. He cursed himself for losing his temper, yet he was prevented from regaining his composure by the memory of ancient injuries, and a crushing sense of impotence in the face of Wickham's lies, which overwhelmed his emotions and overset his thoughts. While he could, and did, pardon Elizabeth for her acceptance of Wickham's lies, whatever they might be, he knew himself to be powerless to combat them. Stiffly following the pattern of the set, he led her through the end of the dance, struggling against his emotions and racking his brain for a way to overcome his dilemma. He blamed himself bitterly, but his thoughts were too undisciplined, and his thoughts on the subject of Wickham too heated, too illiberal, to allow him to express himself judiciously, and he knew he would only make matters worse by speaking aloud what he truly wished to say. Nor did the lady speak, and they finished the dance as they had begun, in silence. He handed her to her seat and left her with a formal bow, and a deep and disturbing sense of something lost.

Chapter Twenty

*A*fter having seated Elizabeth, Darcy had barely time to draw breath before Miss Bingley approached, a malicious and triumphant smile playing about her lips. Linking her arm firmly through his, she said, "Here you are! And so, Mr. Darcy, I see you have finally been so overcome with *ennui* as to make the leap into Hertfordshire society; so good of you—and even before you had had opportunity to dance with your hostess! I am certain the good people of Hertfordshire were highly gratified to see it, as was I! As you *are* my guest, I can wish nothing more than that you should enjoy yourself." Darcy looked down at her rather dejectedly, but made no reply; he had not the strength of will at the moment to engage Miss Bingley in repartée. The lady continued: "And were you well pleased with Miss Elizabeth Bennet as a partner? You seemed very quiet in the last dance, I must say. But perhaps you did not care for the conversation? I can sympathise with you, there; I have just been talking with her sister, who wished to hear every thing she could concerning a certain lieutenant under Colonel Forster; Miss Eliza apparently has a great interest in that quarter."

Darcy, however, was already well aware of that fact, which robbed Miss Bingley of much of her intended effect. She made one or two more attempts to draw him into speech, until, failing to arouse either his curiosity or his ire, she released him and went in search of Elizabeth, as she very much wanted some one whom she might regale to greater effect. Darcy watched her rather dismally as she left him, his emotions in turmoil—charged with frustration, regret, and disgust. His crusade against Wickham had failed; his hopes for the evening were ruined—at least as far as Elizabeth was concerned; he now had a new worry: Bingley and Miss Bennet; and, to make the evening com-

Chapter XX

plete, all his warm hopes, and his best efforts to bring them off, had merely given Miss Bingley a new source of ammunition for her ill-natured teazing. He gave one more look across the room at Elizabeth, fleetingly remembering her hand in his: she would have to do the best she could with Wickham; at least she could not be the object of a serious campaign, he tried to assure himself, as her father's fortune was wholly insufficient to Wickham's needs; and her own goodness and sense would protect her from any attempts at a harmful dalliance, regardless of Wickham's charms. After all, she was not a naïve and open-hearted girl of fifteen, but a clear-sighted young woman who would certainly know how to avoid an imprudent entanglement. With this attempt at reassurance he would have to be satisfied—he could see nothing more that could be done at the moment. He straightened his shoulders and, forcing aside the distraction of his mind, turned his attention to his friend. What was Bingley about, that his affairs were become a matter of open discussion?

"Mr. Darcy?"—a man's voice came just then from his side. Turning, he was surprised to find himself being addressed by that same parson who had so publicly and thoroughly embarrassed Elizabeth during the opening set. He looked first back to Bingley, then reluctantly looked down at this fellow, rather desperately trying to keep his mind clear of the torrent of events that kept thrusting themselves upon his attention.

"Mr. Darcy," the parson repeated with a deep and affected bow, "My name, Sir, is William Collins, and I must apologise most humbly for not having made myself known to you before now—but I have only this moment become aware of the fact that you are related to my most noble patroness, Lady Catherine de Bourgh." Here the man stopped, as though waiting for a reply. Darcy could do nothing but stare at this walking affront to propriety: first he accosts a gentleman unknown to him, then he throws about the name and station of a lady so far above him as to render it an impertinence to claim any knowledge of her. Undeterred by

Darcy's silence, the clergyman went on: "I can assure you, Sir, that your esteemed aunt was in perfect health yesterday se'nnight."

Darcy had heard that his Aunt Catherine had acquired a new parson, and this man appeared to be just the sort of sycophantic fool she would add to her menagerie. Much was explained, though nothing excused. "I thank you for the information," he replied in a cool and dismissive tone; his eyes again sought Bingley and Miss Bennet.

The man refused to take the hint, however, and continued, "Lady Catherine de Bourgh has but lately condescended, with greatest affability, to give me the living in her gift at Hunsford. She has kindly given me leave to come into Hertfordshire to visit the worthy Mr. Bennet — *and* his fair daughters." At the latter portion of this speech the man gave a knowing smirk, as one who would say, "You take my meaning, I'm sure." Darcy, who had reluctantly looked back at him during this speech, at first felt defiled by this too-personal communication, then was thunderstruck by the memory of this fellow's look as he took Elizabeth to the dance floor. He had danced the first two dances with her! Darcy realised with horror that this extraordinarily offensive clergyman had set his sights on Elizabeth! Convinced that the world had gone mad, and that Fate had declared him its plaything, he dared not ask what further evils this evening might hold.

Disgusted with the man — his odd manner, his boorish behaviour to Elizabeth, his effrontery in introducing himself and in sharing a confidence which Darcy would now give a great deal to be ignorant of — he replied with a voice as cold as humanly possible, "I am certain my aunt would never bestow a favour without reason." He did not add, "I imagine she was only too happy to see your back."

Making the mental gesture of shaking off a clinging besmirchment on his person, he turned brusquely away from this odious individual. He walked once about the room to clear his thoughts. Miss Bingley found him during his circuit, and greeted him with a smile of even greater

Chapter XX

malice than the one before: "I see you have met Miss Eliza Bennet's cousin—so pleasant to meet one's future in-laws, is not it? And a parson, too; perhaps he might perform the ceremony! How delightful *that* would be!"

Darcy looked down at her in shock. "I beg your pardon," he replied rather blankly, "I am not sure I take your meaning."

"Why, only that the Reverend Mr. Collins is Miss Eliza's cousin," replied Miss Bingley with a great show of innocence. "Did not you know?"

The clergyman, another relation! Darcy, with a bemusement which left him nearly unable to make sense of his own thoughts, had not the energy to repel Miss Bingley's attack; ceding her victory to her, he withdrew, saying only, "You must not ignore your other guests, Miss Bingley—do not let me keep you." He could not fail to observe the hard satisfaction that glittered in her eyes as he made a brief bow and turned away.

Appalled and reeling from this latest revelation, he recalled that he had only just been wondering what further unpleasantness might await him, and surrendered himself to the irony of receiving such immediate return for having challenged an angry Fate.

His thoughts disordered by too many discoveries coming too quickly together, he roamed vaguely through a number of rooms without attending, deaf to the gaiety around him, until he came upon Bingley and Miss Bennet holding a quiet conversation in a corner of the drawing-room; this brought him back to a sense of purpose, and he determinedly turned his attentions towards his friend. He did so with relief: here, at least, was a problem that was not so directly and pressingly his own; one that he might pursue with a clear mind. A quarter-hour later, however, he could not feel such happy detachment: the degree of attention Bingley devoted to the lady must give pause to all his friends. He had seen Bingley partial to a lady before, but the present case went well beyond any he had observed in the past: so far as Darcy was able to see, Bingley was utterly unaware that he was at a ball, or that he was the host at that ball, or, indeed, that there was any one else about, aside from Miss Bennet. On the lady's side there appeared to be less consuming interest; she smiled pleasantly, as she always did, and certainly Bingley held her attention, but there was a persevering complacency to her air that argued against any great attachment, or, indeed, any great depth of feeling at all.

Having made this observation, Darcy became cautious. He must not rush to judgement on so delicate a matter. If, as he feared, Bingley were to be greatly attached to Miss Bennet, he, Darcy, must be very sure of the lady's regard before venturing to influence his friend. Knowing as he did that his prejudice against the match must colour his judgement, the happiness of his friend, as well as that of the lady, must be protected from injury by an unwarranted officiousness on his part. He therefore bent his powers of observation upon the couple, most seriously endeavouring to gauge the degree of attachment the lady felt for his friend.

There certainly was no want of matter for study, for they almost never parted company. Darcy watched them for at least three quarters of an hour, during which time they engaged in a set of dancing, consumed two cups of punch each (chivalrously fetched by Bingley's hand), and largely ignored six more people who sought to speak with them. The only times, in fact, when others might gain any recognition at all were during those moments when Bingley absented himself from her in search of refreshments; he then became again the host and master of the evening, and she indulged in conversations with her sisters.

Supper soon being served, Darcy followed them into the dining-room and found a seat affording a good view of the couple. Shortly, however, Mrs. Bennet, accompanied by Lady Lucas, sat down directly opposite him. He resigned himself to the aggravation that must arise from her company, however, consoling himself with the thought that whatever vexations he endured would be in the service of

Chapter XX

his friend. Elizabeth followed her mother shortly after and sat on the other side of Lady Lucas, two down from him. Having her near gave him no gratification, however; he had given over any hope in that direction for the evening — Wickham had quite effectively blocked any expectations he might have had for pleasure in that quarter, and, in any event, the question of Bingley's and Miss Bennet's attachment was now become the more grave and weighty matter. He did look Elizabeth's way often enough, but the remnants of that frustration which had ended their dance guarded him from serious thought with regard to her.

While occupied in observing his friend, he could not but overhear Mrs. Bennet's long-winded raptures over the anticipated union, as she, too, dragged his friend's private affairs into public view, describing in glowing and highly audible terms her happiness at the prospect of having Bingley as a son. Her elation was expressed in a loud whisper, which was hardly less than a shout, as she worked to be heard above the clatter of cutlery and the din of scores of conversations. That she was delighted by the possibility was obvious; that she felt all the advantages of the match, revelled in them and gloated over them, was equally obvious. She spoke of Bingley's income with an interest that was only just short of avarice, contemplated the benefits to her younger daughters of moving in circles where they might meet and marry other rich men, and congratulated herself on the nearness of Netherfield to Longbourn. When she declared that the Bingley sisters must desire the connection as much as she did herself, Darcy's expression of amazement and disbelief might have been apparent to his neighbours; how she could remain insensible of Miss Bingley's open disdain for almost the entirety of the Bennet family was beyond comprehension. Indeed, Darcy's contempt and incredulity at the whole of this public display could scarcely be contained, so irritating it was to feelings already fraught with frustration; he did, however, earnestly endeavour to set his jaw and let it pass. But, as her panegyric on the nuptials of her daughter and his friend became more

Into Hertfordshire

and more animated, and more and more lengthy, his disdain overcame his breeding and he allowed his face to reflect his displeasure without disguise.

Poor Elizabeth expostulated repeatedly with her mother, trying to restrain her volubility and, more especially, her volume; but in vain. At one point during such an attempt, Darcy distinguished his own name amongst the hushed syllables of Elizabeth's entreaty. Her mother, with all her usual want of tact, replied aloud: "What is Mr. Darcy to me, pray, that I should be afraid of him? I am sure we owe him no such particular civility as to be obliged to say nothing *he* may not like to hear." While it was hardly possible for Darcy to abominate Mrs. Bennet's manners more than he already did, he almost admired her genius for making herself offensive.

At this direct affront, however, Darcy underwent a sudden shift in disposition; his contempt and disgust changed over to a resolute solemnity of purpose. He had a job of work to do, and an important one: regardless of any other consideration, he must determine whether he was to influence his friend and dissuade him from his pursuit of Miss Bennet. That was the long and short of it. From that point forward did he most strenuously undertake to shut out Mrs. Bennet's effusions: at any rate there could be little left to hear that he had not heard already, and he was certain, with absolute conviction, that she would not be able to best her present mark for ill-bred incivility. There was now before him only the question of being certain of Miss Bennet's relative indifference—or its opposite, her sincere attachment—to his friend.

He continued to observe her most carefully as the couple engaged in conversation; her steady serenity of countenance, whether she spoke with Bingley or with her neighbours, never varied. Having been exposed to the habits of display of innumerable courting couples in the course of nine Seasons in London, he was well aware of the signs to look for, but, try as he might, he could discern no such demonstration of esteem on Miss Bennet's side; she did not

Chapter XX

reach out to touch Bingley's arm as they laughed, her eyes were always kept demurely away from his; even when Bingley faced away from her, Darcy could distinguish no warm glances at him that would bespeak attachment. There was never a moment in which Miss Bennet crossed the bounds of absolute propriety—she might have been at a church bazaar rather than a ball; nor did he ever see any change in her manner when she would turn to one of her neighbours at table, demonstrating that her behaviour to Bingley was in no way different from her behaviour to them. He watched them throughout supper, confirming his observations again and again, until at length he became wholly convinced that Miss Bennet simply could not share Bingley's attachment. To the very best of his ability, he could not see that Miss Bennet distinguished his friend in any way as being more than a pleasant dinner companion. On reaching this conviction, however, his thoughts became even more grave as he considered what must be his course of action. He realised exactly how much this decision must affect his friend's happiness, and the idea of shattering Bingley's hopes tore at Darcy's heart; but, he felt, the head must rule—the heart could not be trusted, certainly not on such a momentous and anxious case as this. He must not let his own disinclination to be the bearer of bad news, dissuade him from protecting his friend's future.

The rest of the evening was largely lost to him, so far as any rewards the social event might offer. As his thoughts were largely consumed by his concerns for his friend, he could do no more than send a regretful glance in Elizabeth's direction from time to time. He did not forget his wishes and intentions where she was concerned, but the unmistakable and immediate danger represented by his friend's attachment held a far more urgent claim on his attention. He was vaguely aware of the fact that the Bennet girl who so loved to exhibit sang an Italian piece, in a weak and reedy voice and an accent that rendered it almost unintelligible, then launched into a second almost before the notably limited applause had ended; he also noticed that her father went so far as to stop her from singing a third, which only served to bring the girl's poor performance to greater attention; nor was he unaware that the odd and odious Mr. Collins continued to make himself an object before the entire party — but these things could gain purchase only on the edges of his mind. His disquiet where the Bennet family was concerned was now centred on the eldest Miss Bennet — the rest would have to wait.

Chapter Twenty-One

After an uncomfortable night, Darcy awoke very unsettled in his thinking; his mind was still clouded and jumbled by that tangle of events and people, which last evening had left him so nearly distracted. Nothing had gone as it should, and now, in hindsight, the one thing he had been grateful for, Wickham's absence, seemed less a blessing; he might at least have faced him down in front of Elizabeth and settled the matter of his lies. But his thoughts eventually arriving at the issue on which he had ended the evening, he recalled his decision, made in the late watches of the night, to deal with Bingley before he left for London: he had an evening appointment there of some importance, and was to leave this morning in order to be in good time.

Casting off the bedclothes he got himself upright with energy; Bingley had intended to leave as soon as he awoke. Ringing the bell for Perkins, he poured water into the ewer and hurriedly washed his face. Barely noticing the chill, he ran a hasty hand through his hair and emerged from his bedchamber just as his man entered. Perkins looked at his master quickly, then set about selecting the day's clothing without comment.

"Perkins," asked Darcy, "do you know if Mr. Bingley is awake?"

"Yes, Sir; Master Bingley was just finishing his breakfast as I was coming up, Sir."

"What! Good Lord! Why must he choose *this* day to become an early riser?"

To this his man offered no reply. Darcy hastily finished dressing and nearly ran down to the breakfast salon to find only the servants clearing and straightening. He moved with haste to the main hall; there he heard voices from without the door. On gaining the stairway to the drive, he

Into Hertfordshire

observed Bingley just in the act of mounting his horse. "Bingley!" he called out.

"Darcy!" His friend, startled to see him, nevertheless offered him one of his smiles. "What brings you out at this hour? I thought to leave before any one else was stirring."

"I am rather surprised to see you about so soon, yourself," replied Darcy. Waving faintly back towards the house, he said, "I was hoping to have a word with you, before you left."

"I *do* have that meeting in Town, and I should hate to be late." Bingley looked curiously at his friend. "What is it?"

Darcy looked at the groomsman holding Bingley's reigns and thought of the footman at the door, both of them new to Bingley's service, and was reluctant to go into the matter in front of them; at Pemberley he was sure of his people, but here? If Perkins might bring information to him, to whom might they convey such matters? His hesitation decided his friend. With a laugh Bingley said, "Well then, as you are undecided—which I can only set down to your having had no coffee as yet—and as I value your good opinion, I shall follow the true Darcy manner and bid you *au revoir*. I shall be back by Saturday, and we shall take it up then." So saying, he urged his horse to a canter and rode off down the drive, still laughing. He called over his shoulder: "If it comes to you, Caroline knows where I will be staying!" Darcy, at a loss, could do no more than watch blankly as he rode away.

Darcy turned reluctant footsteps back to the Hall and the breakfast salon, vaguely but bitterly condemning Wickham for every thing that had gone wrong in the entire week preceding—for it was his arrival, after all, that had touched off this flood of misfortune. He deeply lamented the prior evening's proceedings, but could find nothing to condemn in his own conduct; to him it seemed clear that, without Wickham's lies and interference, the evening would have taken a much different turn.

Chapter XXI

Darcy was still at the breakfast table when Miss Bingley came down. He arose with a bow and prepared to take his leave, being disinclined to share in the enjoyment of assailing the characters and conduct of her guests of the evening before—especially the Bennet family. As he turned to go, however, she reached out a restraining hand. "Pray, do not go, Mr. Darcy," said she. "There is something I must speak to you about." Darcy, caught by the sincerity of her tone, slowly sat back down.

"Mr. Darcy, I am very greatly troubled by my brother's behaviour last evening," she began hesitantly. "I cannot help but think he has allowed himself to become attached...attracted to Miss Bennet."

To this Darcy responded with a solemn nod: "I do not think 'attached' is too strong a word, Miss Bingley. I, too, was aware of his attentions in that direction. Indeed, I believe it was very much discussed throughout the entire company."

"Then you must sympathise with my revulsion at the very idea," she said miserably. "Such a connection would be unendurable! It is not to be thought of!"

"I can agree that the Bennet family, as a whole, cannot be regarded as desirable; but I am the more concerned by the lady's lack of reciprocal feeling," Darcy corrected her mildly. "Your brother is not the sort of man to worry about her connections, or lack thereof, no matter what his friends might think. But when I became aware that their relationship had become the subject of general conversation, I watched them most carefully through the evening; I am sorry to say that I became convinced she does not meet Bingley's affections on an equal footing."

Miss Bingley sniffed disdainfully: "I should not think she cares two figs about him. It is perfectly clear that she *can* only be interested in his position, and his capital."

"There, I cannot agree with you, Miss Bingley," said Darcy even more pointedly. "I have seen nothing in Miss Bennet that bespeaks mercenary tendencies. I see nothing to censure in her behaviour; I merely observe a lack of any special warmth, any particular tenderness towards your brother."

Miss Bingley opened her mouth to retort, but closed it again after a glance at Mr. Darcy. "Of course, you are right, Sir. Miss Bennet is a very sweet and innocent young woman, who can have no thought of material gain through matrimony."

While aware that Miss Bingley's agreement was forced and artificial, Darcy passed it without comment. He said, "The salient point is this: what is to be done about it?"

Miss Bingley's eyes narrowed as she considered. "He will never give over for the sake of his own best interests," she mused aloud.

"Perhaps not," agreed Darcy, "although I should not care to use that phrase in speaking of matrimony to a woman of Miss Bennet's character. But I am very sure that he would never importune a lady, whose affections he had any reason to doubt."

Miss Bingley turned a calculating eye on him. "Precisely!" she cried, after a moment's reflection. "And would you, Mr. Darcy, be willing to give him your observations, your assurances, on that point?"

Darcy admitted without enthusiasm: "I fear I can do no less. I have no wish to be the instrument of his disappointment, but I cannot, as his friend, stand by and let him marry a woman who, no matter how amiable, does not love him as he deserves."

"Oh, Mr. Darcy, you are a true friend!" Miss Bingley cried. "Would that all men could be such as you!" So saying, she leaned over and placed a grateful hand on his.

But in her concurrence and approbation, Darcy found a deep and alarming cause for further doubt, and reason to grow cautious again. Perhaps, he felt, it would be as well to take stock of his observations in the cold light of day. Therefore, withdrawing his hand from hers with a decisiveness that robbed her gesture of its intended warmth, he excused himself that he might review his observations and conclusions in private.

Chapter XXI

Off and on throughout the day, he considered and reconsidered what he had seen, and what he had concluded; but he found nothing to cause him to reverse his decision—other than that he found himself on the same side of the matter as Miss Bingley. Further, when he considered that Bingley and Miss Bennet had known each other less than six weeks, he was persuaded to believe that neither of them could have formed a truly abiding attachment. But there was no time to be lost; if Bingley was to be deflected from this course, it must be done without delay. He must follow his friend to London, and keep him there until his infatuation faded, and the diversions and gaiety of the Season could help him recover from his attachment to Miss Bennet. He did not forget that this would most probably mean there would be no return to Hertfordshire, and that he would likely never see Elizabeth again; but his actions would be the best for every one, and so must mean the least pain for all, in the end. He told himself this several times before his wishes would stop their protests, but he was satisfied with his decision, and was certain *his* feelings, too, would correct themselves, given time.

Late in the afternoon, having made his decision and his plans, he felt called on to attend to his sister, Georgiana; he had not written her since the prior Thursday, when he had sent her a short note in response to her express, stating his intention of staying to the ball as she had requested. He had not then told her of Wickham's presence in the neighbourhood, and its influence on his decision; and he had also yet to tell her the outcome: he only hoped her regrets might be less than his.

Dinner that evening was a nearly silent affair, as each diner was absorbed in thought. That suited Darcy well enough, as the unchecked prattle of the two ladies rarely afforded him any pleasure, and with Bingley away, there was no one to govern their giddy spleen. But on this occasion their thoughts remained fixed on only one topic: what could be done to ward off a connection with the Bennets?

Into Hertfordshire

At length, Darcy rose from the table and said, "I fear I must leave you, Miss Bingley, for London. I do not believe I can defer speaking with your brother until his return; I shall leave first thing to-morrow."

Miss Bingley cast a quick glance at her sister, saying: "But we ought to accompany you, Mr. Darcy, surely. You must not take this wholly upon yourself. And what should we do here alone? For I am certain it would be best if Charles were not to return to Netherfield, at least for some little while. Do not you agree?" To this Darcy bowed his silent acquiescence, and retired to his chambers; there he found Perkins already beginning to pack up his things.

Correspondence

EDITOR'S NOTE

N.B.: It is not necessary to follow the correspondence in its entirety to understand or appreciate the history contained in the body of the work; when important to the movement of the story, the letters, either in part or in whole, have been included in the text. As the written word was so important a means of communication during the time before the advent of electronic communication, though, the letters, even those with no part to play in the story, are included separately to give the reader a chance to follow the story from a different, and perhaps even deeper, perspective, and at a pace more consistent with that experienced by the story's characters.

The correspondence between Mr. Darcy and his sister is given in chronological order by correspondent. The various threads interweave in time, making it all but impossible to follow each thread individually with a proper chronology; it is necessary therefore to separate them in this way. References are given to the appropriate replies, where applicable, to facilitate following the chain of correspondence correctly.

Correspondence

Letters from Miss Georgiana Darcy

*****

*Pemberley
Monday, October 7, —

Dearest Brother,

Thank you for sending Mrs. Annesley to me; she is very gentle and obliging. We spend time every day on my music and reading. Pemberley has been cold since you left, but as I have no wish to go out this is no hardship on me. Colonel Fitzwilliam has stopped in to visit, although you are doubtless already aware of that. He is all kindness, but his solicitude is a constant reminder of my transgressions, and, indeed, I need no such reminder. The Colonel means well, I know, and next to you he is the dearest of my relations, but I do not deserve his concern and my spirits are not sufficient to make me good company. I do not ask a boon, Brother, as I merit none, but I do think my cousin's time would be better spent elsewhere. Perhaps, dear Brother, if you see this as I do, you might suggest to him a different and more worthwhile endeavour? I cannot bear to have him waste his time and care on one such as I.

Your devoted sister,

Georgiana

*For reply, see Darcy, October 10.

*****

*Pemberley
Sunday, November 10, —

Dearest Brother,

Please forgive me for not having written before. I know I am not the correspondent I should be, but please do not think me unappreciative of your letters. My spirits have been low and I have lacked the energy to write; but I have read and re-read your last, for the comfort I find in it is my only support. I carry it with me; indeed, at times I cling to it as a drowning man clings to wreckage.

But you must not think me desperate, and thinking of doing myself an injury. No — I see well enough that those are childish, romantic notions, and I no longer feel myself a child. I have died once for love — it will not happen again. One who has truly known pain would never seek to inflict it on oneself.

Music is my distraction, and Mrs. Annesley recommends that I ride more; I am trying.

Please, dear Brother, write again soon.
Your sister,
Georgiana Darcy

*For reply, see Darcy, November 13.

*****

*Pemberley
Friday, November 15, —

Dearest Fitzwilliam,

Forgive me, please, for not having written this last week, but in truth I feared to do so until I received your reply. I so dreaded your censure; you may imagine my relief, therefore, when…(she struck through this last, and began again). Words cannot say how much it means to me to have your strength to support me. Thank you again and again for the kindness and gentleness of your instruction; you are the most compassionate and generous brother any one might wish for.

What you have written argues strongly with my feelings, and while I am not as accustomed to using logic to guide my life as you are, of course, I own that your arguments appear to me to hold a great deal of truth. Never before had I felt the full force of life's sorrows—not even when Mother and Father passed—but even so I knew I should survive the events of July. Even when I could not see how or why I should live, I knew that I should not succumb to my pain. Until now I had seen this as a punishment; I could not see, as you did, what it must say about eventual recovery.

But while your reassurances are felt more deeply, perhaps, than you can know, in a way it is almost more important to me to know that some one like yourself can possess such acute sensibilities; if not for you and the dear Colonel, I must sometimes despair of there being any feeling among your sex at all. It is hard for me to believe that you and the man who betrayed me are of the same race! How one could be so cruel, yet seem so sweet, and the other be so warm and sensible, yet seem so cool—headed, is beyond my understanding. How will I ever know how to trust, if such a one as he can disguise his true nature so completely? Do we ever learn to distinguish? But no; did not he deceive Father? Oh, Fitzwilliam, tell me how I shall ever trust again!

No; I must not let my feelings distort my thoughts—pray forgive my lapse. My doubts press upon me too strongly at times, but it passes. There *is* truth and warmth among my fellow creatures—in my family there is, I know: you, the Colonel, dear Aunt Eleanor and Uncle Jonathan, these are my proofs. I must hold firmly to these, and barricade my heart against the rest. My family shall be my bastion and my talisman. There, it shall be so. Yes; I have my anchor, and I shall no longer be tossed about in the storm. I shall learn to be myself again, I promise you, dear Brother.

Your idea of impoverishing the family I found inexpressibly shocking, Fitzwilliam; I am mortified by the very notion. I should not have thought it possible that you might be so sensible of my condition as to even imagine such a thing. I could never allow you to take any step that might injure our family further on my behalf. You must never think on this subject again. I am very aware of the trouble I have been, and I am ashamed to have caused you such difficulty and distress; I know it must have cost you a great deal to write on such distasteful matters without giving way to a very natural abhorrence. Your clear-headedness amazes me; I am not yet able to keep my despair from intruding into my calmer thoughts, although I am trying with each day to push it farther from me. Your composure in dealing with these matters will be my model, and I shall try with every day to gain a better mastery over myself.

Do not concern yourself by your absence; I need reflection more than diversion. Do not, therefore, leave your friends on my account. Know, too, that I would not hesitate to call you home if there were need; but though there are times, I confess, that I would be glad of the sight of you (never more than at this moment, dear Brother), I still feel as I did before: that it is best that I have this time to myself.

Tell me more of Mr. Bingley's 'country miss,' and her sister—I have never heard you speak so

Correspondence

of a woman; she must be beyond amiable to have earned your approbation. You approve of her conversation and countenance, but what is she like? Is she kind? She is there to care for her sister, so I assume she must be a good-hearted lady. What are her accomplishments? What is it about her that has won your good opinion? You must write more fully.

In closing let me thank you again, Brother dear, not so much for your letter as for being yourself. I feel most fortunate, yet so undeserving, to have your love and care.

Yours, most truly,
Georgiana Darcy

*For reply, see Darcy, November 18.

*****

*Pemberley
Saturday, November 16, —

Dearest Fitzwilliam,

It is you who honour me with your trust, dear Brother—how you can continue to extend it to me surpasses my understanding; I am deeply sensible that I have forfeited any right to expect it, but I am so very, very grateful to have it. As for forgiving you for your unreserve, there can be no need, surely; having already placed myself in the midst of scandal, I can hardly be offended by your composure and openness in advising me on how it might be dealt with. How could I object to your words, when they do but speak to my actions? And to suggest that it might be in my power to forgive you, you who have been so blessedly forgiving to me, makes me feel all the more deeply how little worthy I am to do so.

I do not view what you wrote as lecturing, you must never think that; I welcome your thoughts from my heart. My feelings, indeed, have so clouded my abilities, crowding out reason and calm deliberation, that having your abilities to rely on is a great relief to me. To know that your words still hold true after a day's deliberation is most reassuring. But there is one thing I do know full well, Brother; you must give over your attempts to take the blame for my actions upon yourself. It was not your inattention, but my foolish heart, that led me to my present discreditable state. If we allow ourselves to let others take the blame for our misdeeds, where would it end? No; if my reflections have led me to any truth, it is that my own weakness and foolish, romantic inclinations were responsible for my naïve faith in his lies and flattery. I allowed his persuasions to lull to sleep that sense of duty which told me I was acting wrongly.

That is, indeed, my present dilemma: I know wherein lies my mistake — what I do not know is how I can ever come to trust my feelings again. If the deepest feelings of one's heart can be so much in error, what hope is there of ever finding contentment in life? This is the question I struggle with daily; for without contentment, without happiness and hope for the future, what is life? But I shall desist; I do not wish to dwell on these thoughts nor bore you with the seemingly endless variations on them that are my constant companions.

I found your comments on Miss Bingley to be most amusing: I am sure she would be mortified to know what you write, and, as I have told

Correspondence

you before, you must be very careful not to permit your letters to be seen, even briefly and by hazard, lest you offend your friend's nearest relations.

Poor Miss Elizabeth Bennet! To be burdened with such a mother, yet to possess such resources of wit and humour! What you have written is wonderful to me: you have never before spoken so highly, nor at such length, of any woman in your acquaintance. I should dearly like to meet her, Brother, truly I should. Does she go to Town? Do you imagine she might come to Derbyshire? Has she any friends near Pemberley? Do please enquire, Fitzwilliam, for my sake, if not for yours.

You spoke of Miss Bennet's sister, in your previous letter, as being from a family of "little standing and no connections." But their father is a gentleman, surely? I cannot imagine Miss Bingley stooping so far below her class in seeking companionship as to befriend any one from any other station. I am confused by what you have written; most especially by what you describe as Miss Bingley's "quest for ascendancy" over Miss Bennet. Surely, if their stations were so dissimilar, this would not occur: Miss Bingley's standing would secure her from the need to vie with Miss Bennet. Yet you believe Miss Bennet would not be accepted by...whom? The rest of your acquaintance, or perhaps your relations? In Town, or in Derbyshire? But how could she hold forth with you on such diverse matters if she felt herself your inferior? And why would she not dance with you? I cannot resolve this; you must write more particularly when you receive this.

Notwithstanding, you sound as if you are enjoying your stay in Hertfordshire, and I am very glad of that. I look forward to your next letter.
Your loving sister,
Georgiana Darcy

*For reply, see Darcy, November 19.

*****

*Pemberley
Sunday, November 17, —

Dearest Fitzwilliam,

Thank you for your letter of the 15th; I find your descriptions of what passes at Netherfield a most welcome diversion. What you write about Miss Bingley, unfortunately, does not surprise me as much as it should; in all truth I must confess that I have found in her an unfortunate tendency towards assurance, self-indulgence, and a certain coarseness of feeling; I hope you will forgive me for speaking so of some one of your acquaintance, but I believe this to be a very serious matter, and I would have you know what I know. I have heard her speaking with her sister in unguarded moments when there were no members of the opposite sex present, and observed in her a most…pragmatic…view of men. She counts herself among the most eligible women in London Society, and she is bent on making a "conquest worthy of her qualities," to use her expression; it would appear that she finds you worthy. I need hardly say, but be most circumspect, Brother. She is capable of stratagems that make me blush to contemplate. Time, and an adamantine adherence

Correspondence

to propriety, will eventually discourage her, as she knows that youth is fleeting, and desires to make her "conquest" before her bloom is gone.

But let me pass on to a more agreeable topic: I am most desirous of knowing more of Miss Elizabeth Bennet; what you have written interests me greatly. Brother, you have confused me exceedingly, for you say on the one hand that she is all that is amiable, and on the other that any connection with her family is unthinkable; yet you have never said *why*. As you know, I am forced to conclude that she is a gentleman's daughter, by her inclusion in the Netherfield family circle. What, then, is the impediment? You have mentioned her nonsensical mother, but it cannot be this, because, well...good Heavens, if one were to name all of the nonsensical mothers in London, or in Derbyshire, for that matter—and certainly in Kent—the list would be formidable, indeed.

And I am very troubled to hear that you will leave before the ball; pray do not—please? We shall be amply prepared for our relations' visit without your hurrying your departure. Will you not stay to dance with Miss Bennet? I would have you do so, dear Brother, truly I would. It would be a shame indeed if you were to lose her acquaintance forever without ever once having danced with her.

I have already begun preparations for our removal to Town. Mrs. Annesley and I have discussed what is needful, and have already planned several possible entertainments for the time our family is all together; so you see, Fitzwilliam, there is no need for you to hurry your return.

I shall hope to hear that you have changed your mind, and decided to stay, when I receive your next letter.
Your affectionate sister,
Georgiana Darcy

*****

*Pemberley
Wednesday, November 20, —

Dearest Fitzwilliam,

Have no fear, Brother, on receiving this letter by express, lest it contain ill-tidings; all is well here at Pemberley. It is only that I read with great disappointment in your last that you are definitely planning to leave Netherfield before Mr. Bingley's ball, and I was compelled to write you before this plan should be carried out. Why must you leave without attending the ball, Fitzwilliam? The idea that you will leave Miss Elizabeth Bennet behind you without ever having danced with her, quite breaks my heart. At the very least you must allow yourself to take her hand for one dance.

You see, as it happens, I was not so very surprised by the intelligence you offered in your letter, to the effect that you had found yourself attracted to Miss Bennet; inasmuch as she is the only lady you have ever distinguished to me by any degree of approbation, and since you have so distinguished her in each one of your letters since you met her, your admission comes too late for surprise. All that you have written to me of her has quite delighted me, Fitzwilliam, and I wish most earnestly to meet her. But, as you will know when you have received my earlier letters, I am at

Correspondence

a loss to understand your objections to her. Surely her family's standing cannot be so far beneath our own as to forbid you even to feel for her, or she would never be admitted as a guest into Mr. Bingley's house. I would never presume to think you mistaken, but I would most sincerely wish to understand your thoughts more fully. And I hope you will forgive the question, my dear Brother, but are you sure that in deciding this you have also listened to your heart? That the heart and mind must always follow the same pole-star is not true, of course; but neither does it follow that the path chosen by the heart is *always* the wrong one.

But never mind *my* opinions on *your* heart; they mean little enough, indeed—you recently entreated me, though, to tell you if there was anything whatever that would give me pleasure, and I now ask this of you, Fitzwilliam: to gratify *my* heart, would you please stay to the ball, and dance with Miss Bennet? Please, for my sake? I can hardly explain why it should be so, but this means a great deal to me, and I do hope you will find it in your power to indulge me in this.

Your loving sister,
Georgiana Darcy

*For reply, see Darcy, November 21.

*****

Pemberley
Saturday, November 23, —

Dearest Fitzwilliam,

I hope all is well; your letter made it sound almost as if you were distressed over some of your affairs. I hope this is not true, and that your time in Hertfordshire remains pleasurable.

I am so very glad that you have decided to stay—I thank you from my heart for indulging me in this way. I hope and trust you will be happy you took the opportunity to dance with Miss Bennet, and I am sure you will find her to be a charming partner. I dare say I am as excited as you—possibly more—at the idea. I shall look forward very much to hearing all the details of your evening.

I imagine Mr. Bingley's ball room to be rather like ours; perhaps a little smaller, but that would make for a delightfully hospitable setting, I should think. I cannot suppose the country neighbourhood could supply more than forty or fifty couples, although the proximity of Netherfield to London might make it possible for some to come in especially, I suppose. In any event, knowing Miss Bingley as I do, I am certain it will all be done most thoroughly, and no detail will be ignored.

Oh, Fitzwilliam!—you have made me very happy! Have you had occasion yet to ask Miss Bennet if she is to be in Town at all this winter? Or if she ever comes into Derbyshire? You must try to remember to do so.

Well, I am sure I shall have an hundred questions to ask you after, but for now I shall say good-bye, as I calculate that this will just reach you before the ball; I shall leave off now to post it. I pray the ball will answer all your hopes, and I remain,
Your affectionate—and grateful—sister,
Georgiana Darcy

*****

Correspondence

Letters from Mr. Fitzwilliam Darcy

*****

Grosvenor Square
Thursday, October 10, —

Dearest Sister,

My dear, gentle Georgiana, your letter grieves me more than words can express. Your pain is my doing, entirely; I neglected you and trusted others to perform duties that properly belonged to me. Mrs. Younge abused my trust while you were at Ramsgate, it is true; but she could not have done so had not I, with an imprudence altogether inexcusable in one of my years, accepted her recommendations without sufficient enquiry. Nor had I prepared you as I ought to have done for such men as he. I knew him for what he was, yet never sought to inform you, not only of *his* character, but even of the existence of such predatory men. My excuse is that I had thought to preserve your innocence and spare you this knowledge, but I see now that that is like sparing the knowledge of fire: we encounter it every where, and if we are not taught caution it will do us a grave injury. My Mother, I know, would not have left you defenceless in this way, and I berate myself for not having foreseen this need. I, who pride myself on my understanding, have failed utterly in its application.

I have allowed you to be badly burned, and I pray to God that the pain will subside and the

scars will fade, for yours is the sweetest nature Heaven ever sent to Earth; if I have allowed such an angelic disposition to suffer permanent damage I shall never forgive myself. Dearest, you must believe me: you did no more than accept the lies of a man who could deceive even one so worthy as Father, as you must now realise he was wholly deceived by the man. And you must remember, as I certainly do, that it was your own goodness that made you acknowledge to me your planned elopement, for the pain you knew it would give me. You are too good: you cannot allow even your most pressing desires to harm another. Please, please consider my words, Dearest, and believe that I am,
Your most loving and contrite brother,
Fitzwilliam Darcy

*****

*Netherfield Park, Herts.
Wednesday, November 13, —

My dearest Georgiana,

I promise I shall write to you every day, now I know you wish for my correspondence. And do not feel burdened by the need to reply; do so at your convenience, and if you have anything to say.

Dearest, are you sure that I had not better be at home with you? There is nothing here that requires my presence, and even if there were, nothing could take precedence over your slightest needs. Tell me instantly if you want me, and I shall be home before the sun rises twice.

Correspondence

Though I have no experience with a betrayal as deep as the one you have suffered, I do know that even the deepest wounds must heal in time, if we can but survive the initial blow. This you have done, and what is more, you have *felt* this to be true, which is infinitely more important than being *told*, no matter by whom. I refer to your realization that harming yourself is not a solution. Pain so great as to overwhelm the mind and body can, most assuredly, result from such injuries as yours. *Felo de se*, in these cases, is no more than a delayed reaction to the original attack; that you do not feel such an exigence is proof that you have not taken mortal injury. This is why I can confidently say that you will heal. You may not have had these thoughts in mind when you wrote me those lines, but, perhaps, now that I have presented them in this light you might see them as I do. And you ought to know that I was never alarmed by any thought of your doing yourself an injury; I knew you would never have done anything rash, for I know you. Whether you made a deliberate decision, or were simply acting according to your nature, I was certain that you could never conduct yourself in a way that would harm others, as such an act must invariably do.

So, given time, you must heal. Not to the degree that you will ever be exactly the same as you were before, I know, and that saddens me immeasurably; but neither will you be crippled by the scars—that I swear. It was I who failed to protect you, and it is upon me to see to your recovery. If the path to restoring your strength leads us to the ends of the earth, if I must ransom our lands and impoverish every one of our connections, I will see you whole again. Please, Dearest, please do not hold back if there is anything you want, anything you desire, anything that holds even the faintest hope of cheering you.

Now, let me tell you the news from here. Mr. Bingley has, seemingly, managed yet again to stumble into a pleasant situation; his propensity for leaping blindly is surpassed only by his great good fortune in not cracking his noggin on landing. With no more than half-an-hour's investigation, he has managed to secure a lovely estate. Of course, Hertfordshire is not Derbyshire, but still and all it is handsome and well-suited to his needs. Miss Bingley and Mr. and Mrs. Hurst are here with us, so Miss Bingley has a willing audience for her wit and there is no want of loo and whist. Mr. Bingley is smitten again, this time with a country miss of little standing and no connections, but a lovely girl nonetheless, whose smiles are the only ones I have ever seen that outshine Bingley's own. She also is here, owing to having been taken ill during a visit to Miss Bingley. She is attended by one of her sisters, whose conversation and countenance have been among the brighter notes of this expedition into the country. But now, Dearest, I must leave off to post this and go down to dinner. I promise to write more fully to-morrow. Until then, know that you are in my heart and thoughts.

Your devoted, albeit distant, brother,
Fitzwilliam Darcy

*For reply, see Georgiana, November 15.

*****

Correspondence

*Netherfield Hall
Thursday, November 14, —

Dearest Georgiana,

I hope you have had time to read and reflect on my letter of yesterday; as I think back on it I can find no part of it that I would amend. I trust you will forgive me for writing so openly and feelingly on such subjects, knowing as you do that I should never write so to another. But with you I have no reservations, nor do I fear that I might be misunderstood, as you will always honour me with the benefit of your trust and your good heart. But as I have no desire to lecture on these topics, I shall henceforth hold my thoughts on the subject in abeyance, until you have had an opportunity to reply.

Miss Bingley here asks that I convey to you her compliments, and her delight in the prospect of seeing you at Christmas. We are in the drawing-room after dinner; she sits near me as I write, and sanctions my efforts with her fullest approval and encouragement. If, therefore, my letter seems stilted or haphazard in its construction, or some tinge of exasperation creeps into it, I pray you will forgive me and attribute it to the appropriate cause.

While here at Netherfield I have encountered rare new levels of both sense and nonsense; here I have met with one whose nonsensical views and mental dishevelment surpasses any other in my experience. This is one Mrs. Bennet, who is mother to the two young ladies I told you of yesterday. She is a veritable caricature of unreason, unable to hold onto a single thought long enough to complete an intelligible sentence, and yet at the same time maintaining a complete assurance of the sagacity of her judgement and the rectitude of her opinions. I have been in her company now several times, and never once has she offered a comment worth the hearing. Her two eldest daughters, I am happy to say, the ones who are staying presently at Netherfield Hall, have escaped the misfortune of sharing their mother's affliction. She has three other daughters, however, who are certainly infected with the disorder, although not to such an acute degree.

Notwithstanding, the second Miss Bennet, Miss Elizabeth Bennet, is that very one whose sense and understanding is so superior to any other lady's in my acquaintance. She has just joined us in the drawing-room after tending to her sister throughout the day, and most of the night prior. Save for you, she shows the greatest good sense and warmest regard for others I have ever seen combined in any of my fellow creatures.

Between Miss Bennet and Miss Bingley there exists a great disparity of personality, and I have been afforded no small measure of entertainment by studying the difference between Country manners and Town manners. Miss Bingley is every inch the Society Miss, as you know, having lived almost exclusively in London, whereas Miss Bennet's manners have nothing fashionable about them — she, as I believe, having been brought up largely here in Hertfordshire. It is interesting to contrast her character and Miss Bingley's: she is sincere where Miss Bingley is witty, witty where Miss Bingley is affected, charming where Miss Bingley is smart, warm where Miss Bingley is well-mannered. And Miss Bennet is possessed of a singular intellect: I have seen her run verbal circles around a staunch military man, yet show such rare concern and compassion as to do so without giving him so much as a hint of what she was about, and taking no advantage of the poor man at all. Upon your brother she has turned her wit like unto a well-honed rapier, and yet has done so in the most charming manner imaginable. She is very amiable, and adores dancing (although, to say the truth, she has turned down my hand), and even though the society hereabouts offers little by comparison with her own talents, she remains thoroughly modest, unaffected by the awareness she could scarcely avoid of her own superior gifts.

I must diverge again, as Miss Bingley, having earlier commended the speed and evenness of my writing, now wishes me to convey to you her "raptures" over the design for a table you made last summer, to express how delighted she is to hear of your improvement in music (forgive me; I must confess that I often boast about you), and diverse other expressions of esteem. In truth, Dearest, I am not certain whether all this is meant for you, or even me; I suspect that it may have to do with Miss Bingley's quest for ascendancy over Miss Bennet. Her display of approbation may be nothing more than a form of boast; making mention of such things as an indication of the superior society in which she travels, and to which Miss Bennet could have no access at all.

All this gives me to feel how fortunate you and I have been to be raised in Derbyshire, and yet to have had frequent access to Town; for the Country holds England's heart, while London is the seat of its intellect and initiative. We therefore have the best of both worlds: the heart to know what is good and right, and the head to seek and to savour it.

I have been drawn off again, Dearest, by a most agreeable interlude. Miss Bingley began it with another commendation of my letter, and her brother, who is, I gather, just as tired as I am of her perpetual compliments, took the opportunity to get in a dig at me to balance matters up. Miss Bingley came to my defence immediately, and Miss Bennet took up Bingley's cause. I do not know where Miss Bennet was educated (surely not in Hertfordshire), but she is highly accomplished in debate and logic. She managed to turn a comment Bingley made on his untidy habits of thought into a testament to his humility. Now, Bingley has many excellent qualities, but on my honour, humility is not one of them: he is proud enough of his accomplishments — his natural modesty lies in the fact that he simply fails to recognise many of them. He would allow her interpretation to stand, however, being well-pleased to stand in borrowed glory. I returned his dig with interest, pointing out how deceitful false humility must be. I had him fairly cornered when his advocate came to his rescue. But she quickly outran his wit and he dropt out of the race, as his sister had done even earlier, leaving the two of us to finish the course; but, alas, in his amiability and the equanimity of his humour, Bingley does not appreciate the delights of active discourse, and felt Miss Bennet and I were perhaps too much in earnest in our dispute. He dissuaded me from continuing, drawing on his privilege as my friend to call a halt to the clash of our reasoning without the others' knowledge. I obliged him, of course: even if I did not hold him in such high regard, as a guest I could never be disobliging to my host; but I confess I have never been half so well entertained in this house before. Miss Bennet has dismissed me to "finish my letter," and so I shall,

Correspondence

Dearest. I am hopeful of hearing from you soon, and I remain,
Your loving brother,
Fitzwilliam Darcy

*For reply, see Georgiana, November 16.

*****

*Netherfield Hall
Friday, November 15, —

My dear Georgiana,

    I have ensconced myself in my chambers this afternoon, as I feel a need for solitude not unlike your own. Even when one is genuinely fond of one's companions, there are times when nothing is better suited to a contemplative nature than a period of quietude and solitary repose. Little has changed since my letter yesterday, except, perhaps, that Miss Bingley has been more trying than usual. I have told you before that I suspected her of entertaining hopes of becoming mistress of Pemberley, and my stay in Hertfordshire has, if anything, added to that conviction. She has, on numerous occasions, attempted to increase the intimacy of our acquaintance to a degree I could never allow. I shall give you one example, although there have been many, as this instance struck me with particular force: on the occasion of an assembly here in the village, Miss Bingley actually sent her maid to Perkins with directions as to my attire, that I might match her own. I can imagine your surprise at such impertinence, and I heartily agree—I was never more affronted; beyond that, however, I see in this presumption of privilege an attempt to persuade either herself, or me, or all parties concerned, that we are on terms. That I have never given any hint of willingness to be on terms with Miss Bingley goes without saying, yet here is my dilemma: how can I dissuade her and bring about a cessation of these intrigues and machinations without causing pain or offense to my friend? You know my feelings on deceit and the evils it brings: I hereby add guile and duplicity to the list of things I abhor.

In addition, it was borne in upon me to-day that Miss Bingley might harbour some feelings of jealousy with regard to myself; and towards Miss Elizabeth Bennet, of all people. I freely admit that I admire Miss Bennet's wit and humour, but there can never be more than that between us, obviously. The pain afforded to Miss Bingley by this jealousy would count for little, as it is of her own making, but she is disobliging and ill-mannered to Miss Bennet as well, which, to my mind, shows an unconscionable lack of good breeding. The manner in which ladies contest with their tongues I find most vexatious; although I will say that Miss Bennet never stoops to any such sign of ill-breeding—at least, she has never done so in my presence, and Miss Bingley has offered her numerous opportunities for such a display of pique. But perhaps I am too severe on my fellow creatures. Men are more formally civil than women in their dealings with one another, I believe, for among men harsh or disobliging words lead to anger and swift blows: the matter is either settled directly, or it may, in extreme cases, be necessary to resort to a challenge. But women, having no such ready release for their antipathies, must find other means of contestation. Or, looking at the same phenomenon from an entirely different viewpoint, perhaps we men are simply more easily offended than women, and in our contumacious natures we have no restraints to keep us from violence, so we practise civility the more diligently simply to keep ourselves from each other's throats. It is an interesting question, and I am sure it would take a wiser man than I to resolve it. What I do know with certainty is that if any man had behaved towards me the way Miss Bingley has towards Miss Elizabeth Bennet, I should have no alternative but to call him out.

The weather here has been seasonable and there has been some sport, but much of our time has been spent within doors. I am beginning to believe it is time that I thought of returning to London, and thence home to escort you to Grosvenor Square for the winter Season. Bingley contemplates giving a ball within a fortnight, so I have that much more reason to absent myself from Hertfordshire.

Well, I have, I believe, bored you with my small affairs long enough, and so I shall close, Dearest. Know that you are always in my thoughts, and that I remain,
Your loving brother,
Fitzwilliam Darcy

*For reply, see Georgiana, November 17.

*****

Netherfield Hall
Saturday, November 16, —

My dearest Georgiana,

To-day was rather uneventful here in Hertfordshire; we have heard that the Bennet sisters are to leave us to-morrow. Bingley has tried on several occasion to persuade Miss Bennet that her health is not yet sufficiently recovered to risk the journey of three miles back to her father's estate, but he has failed to convince her; she is right, of course: it is merely that Bingley is loath to give up her company. I have never seen any one who could fall in love so easily as my friend, yet he never seems to leave behind any ill-feelings when the sentiment fades. The ladies he has distinguished with his short-lived regard, and their relations as well, all seem perfectly happy to continue his acquaintance: the worst I have seen is a degree of wistfulness in their treatment of him. Yet I would never think him a shallow person: I do believe his feelings are deep enough; his regard for Miss Bennet most certainly is, to judge by his attentiveness to her during her illness, and in his sincere attempts to keep her here with us. It is not depth his attractions lack: it is permanence. Perhaps this is the nature of love from the heart: as it can appear suddenly, it can be gone just as quickly. The love that has survived the test of one's higher powers must surely withstand the test of time, as well.

As I said, little has happened here to-day, and I have begun to turn my thoughts towards the holidays, and away from Hertfordshire. Indeed, I have already done so to the degree that I spoke hardly a word to-day to Miss Elizabeth Bennet, or to her sister either, that I recall. I have written to the Colonel to confirm our holiday plans, so I believe we may expect our relations on the 19th, as planned; I am very much looking forward to seeing them — not excepting even Cousin George, although I could hardly tell you why; but there it is: I am actually looking forward to a visit from the Viscount Saint Stephens.

Correspondence

I am much more earnestly looking forward to seeing you, Dearest, and hearing all about the plans you have been making. I have had a note from Goodwin hinting that we shall have a very full calendar leading up to Christmas, but—on your orders, it appears! —he declines to give me any details. I intend to arrive at Pemberley on the 11th to escort you to Town, at which time I trust you will allow me into your confidence, you sly thing! Suborning my own servants, and from the other end of the kingdom, no less! I had no idea you were that devious. But I will say that I have made no fixed engagements, meaning to keep my schedule open to accommodate your plans, whatever they might be.

And so, Dearest, that exhausts my information, I believe, so I shall bring this to an end. I remain,
Your loving brother,
Fitzwilliam Darcy

*****

*Netherfield
Sunday, November 17, —

Dearest Georgiana,

I am rather fatigued, as the time to-day seemed to drag on interminably, so this will be shorter than I might wish. The Misses Bennet left us to-day after Morning Services, and the effort to maintain a decent level of conversation in their absence has been painfully great. Bingley was, of course, much saddened by Miss Bennet's departure, which left his spirits low. Miss Bingley, on the other hand, was in very high spirits indeed after they left, but her conversation I found to be monotonous, as she never wavered from heaping scorn and abuse on her two erstwhile guests.

Will it surprise you, Dearest, if I tell you that I found myself on the verge of an attraction for Miss Elizabeth Bennet? It is true. But be assured; I may have loosed the reins, but I did not fall off. I was most careful to shield Miss Bennet from any knowledge of my feelings; I never even took her hand for a dance—no, that is not entirely accurate: rather, I would have to admit that she never accepted my hand for a dance—but perhaps I might have mentioned that before. In any event, she is gone, and I am reasonably well assured that she has no idea of having ever excited my interest.

I must say, though, now that she is no longer before me, that it has occurred to me to wonder at the fact that after so many Seasons in London the only woman ever to have captured my attention should be so impossibly distant from me in standing. Why, of the literally hundreds of women to whom I have been introduced, should the only one whose acquaintance is worth the having—for me, personally, that is—be so little esteemed in the eyes of Society? It puzzles me; upon my honour, it does puzzle me.

I have put any feelings I might have harboured for her behind me, of course. I could not in honour, in civility, in faith, distinguish her at all—there could be no hope of an alliance, and such feelings as I may have had for her served no purpose other than to bring discomfort to the bearer of them. I own, however, that it has long appeared to me that the impish sports of Fate seem peculiarly to conspire against the wishes of men, giving us glimpses only of what felicity might be, then arranging the world so that no such happy lot can ever be ours. But come, I must not be self-pitying: I doubt not that there are very few in the whole of England who would feel that Darcy of Pemberley was in need of sympathy; one must always keep one's perspective.

Bingley, as I mentioned, was downcast (for him, that is) by the departure of Miss Bennet, but he has cheered himself up with thoughts of the ball he plans this Tuesday week. With this diversion to occupy him, and with the expectation of dancing a set—or might we suspect that he intends to dance even more than one?—with the beguiling Miss Bennet, he will have no trouble supporting his spirits. I have not yet spoken to him, but I do not intend to stay to it; there would be no purpose and I would just as soon begin my journey to Pemberley. My current plans are to leave this Saturday for Town, then set off for home next Tuesday week, as I mentioned before. I am counting the days until I shall be with you again.

Your loving—and homeward turning—brother,
Fitzwilliam Darcy

*For reply, see Georgiana, November 20.

*****

Netherfield
Monday, November 18, —

My dearest Georgiana,

I have received your letter of the 15th. Do not concern yourself about your performance as a correspondent; such replies as you are moved to make are ample reward for my efforts—I have no need of daily communication from your side. And, forgive me for contradicting you, but you are by no means undeserving; rather it is I who am blest with so good and so caring a sister.

It is, Dearest, very difficult indeed to know who is good and who is false in this life. I believe that one of the most important functions of family is to preserve one another from those pernicious influences to be found in the world, and to help each other recover from our encounters with them. Be not disturbed, then, by any thought of imposition arising from my attentions to your needs. There can be no imposition or obligation in having those close to your heart be concerned on your behalf; and if God grants us both time enough, I assure you that there will come a time when I shall want your help on my behalf. I believe, as you have come to do, that one's family is, or ought to be, the strong fortress and the safe haven against the world's evils, and I thank Heaven that ours is as it is, and can serve us well in that capacity.

I am very pleased that you found my thoughts useful. But whether one follows the dictates of logic or not, one must not let one's apprehensions cloud the mind, nor yet the heart. Not all the world is bad, no more than every dog is vicious or every blaze on the hearth is a conflagration in the making. With most of Nature's dangers, however, we can see them for what they are; it is only our own ill-wrought and unnatural species that is capable of dissemblance, and it is therefore our lot to face the necessity of distinguishing the good from the bad. I do most firmly believe that the intent to lie is at the heart of every sin Man has ever committed, and my abhorrence of guile and mendacity in all its aspects rests on that conviction. But I am mindful, Dearest, that for every deceitful man, we find also a Bingley, who is every bit as true as your betrayer is false, as honourable as he is depraved, and as open-hearted as he is selfish.

As you will have found by the time this reaches you, I have already written at greater length about the Misses Bennet. They left Netherfield yesterday, and, while the loss of their conversation took with it most of the substance of our evening conversations, all in all it is just as well that they are gone; well, perhaps not the elder Miss Bennet, as the sweetness of her disposition made a welcome amendment to the sometimes acerbic nature of Bingley's sisters.

Miss Elizabeth Bennet is, indeed, a singular young woman; but, as I wrote to you on Sunday, I enjoyed her company more than was good for either of us. The differences in our circumstances make it impossible that we should be more than acquaintances, and I have no wish to cause pain either to her or myself by imagining that it might be otherwise. It was therefore necessary and…well, not desirable, precisely—but certainly best for all, that our association end.

I have written to the Colonel to confirm our plans for the holiday season, and I am sure you will be glad to see our Aunt and Uncle again, as will I. When last I heard it was uncertain whether Lord Saint Stephen would accompany them, as it was thought his affairs in Town might be too pressing for him to attend more than an evening or two. That exhausts my present information, and so, dear Sister, I shall bid you adieu.

Your loving brother,

Fitzwilliam Darcy

*****

Netherfield
Tuesday, November 19, —

Dearest Georgiana,

I have just read yours of the 16th, and where you question how contentment is to be found, when the heart is so little to be trusted, is one of my own great quandaries of the last year and more. You know my dedication to logic and the intellect: as I have touched on before, to be able to love and esteem with the mind is, I believe, much more difficult than to love with the heart, as the heart requires no proofs of worthiness to love. The heart can accept an object of love with as little as one look at that object, if we are to believe the romantic version of love that abounds in literature; but the mind must take longer: it must be convinced again and again, and belief must wait on many proofs in many guises, before it can be admitted. How then can one expect to love with both the heart and the mind; the two work within such different periods of time, how can they ever harmonise? Yet one without the other is only half a love, surely. But I regret that I have no answer for you, and I would have left the topic alone entirely, except that I wished to let you know that you were not alone in your dilemma.

I agree with you that it is, indeed, a shame that Miss Elizabeth Bennet's relations are what they are; her mother stands alone in my memory for her ill-founded assurance and ill-bred impropriety. And speaking of impropriety, I must say Miss Bingley's disobliging behaviour to Miss Bennet is nonsensical to me. I cannot say why she feels the need to compete with her: in the first

Correspondence

place, I will never make my addresses to Miss Bingley; in the second, it is obvious that there can be no alliance between Miss Bennet and myself, so Miss Bingley's jealousy is completely misplaced.

How Miss Bennet will fare in future concerns me as well, or it would if I had any right to interest myself in her future. But my only contribution to it must be wholly negative in nature: I can only protect her from the ill-effects of my own regard for her — there is nothing I can do to correct her situation, nor have I any right to make the attempt.

Well, Dearest, I have been writing this in the breakfast salon while I waited for the others to come down, and I begin to hear stirrings from above. I shall therefore leave off to post this before any one arrives. I am, truly,
Your loving brother,
Fitzwilliam Darcy

*****

*Netherfield
Thursday, November 21, —

Dearest Georgiana,

This will only be a note, as I have a complex and delicate issue under consideration; I just want you to know that I have received your express, and I shall stay to the ball as you ask. I shall write more fully when I am able — but do not be alarmed if you do not hear from me for some little while, as I foresee that during this next week my attentions might be fully engaged. Meanwhile, know that you are in my thoughts and heart. God bless you and keep you safe,
Your loving brother,

Fitzwilliam Darcy

*For reply, see Georgiana, November 23.

*****

Netherfield
Wednesday, November 27, —

Dear Georgiana,

Well, we have had our ball. It began well enough, though it was not until the third set that I could secure Miss Bennet's hand. As you predicted, I was very well pleased to stand up with her. But I regret to say that the evening was not to end as well as it began.

To begin with, I had a worry I did not share with you in my last—something I wish I did not have to report: I have again seen the man who betrayed you. He has but recently joined the regiment stationed here in Meryton, and, owing to Mr. Bingley's ignorance of the fact, he was included in the invitation issued to the officers of that corps. I confess that this had an influence on my decision to stay, as I hoped to give Miss Elizabeth Bennet some measure of warning about the man. While he thankfully did not attend the ball, I fear he has in some way already garnered Miss Elizabeth Bennet's good opinion; this had a rather dampening effect on the time I spent with her.

This was not the only circumstance which interfered with my hopes for the evening, however, nor even the most pressing: my attentions were drawn away from Miss Elizabeth Bennet perforce, as it appears Mr. Bingley has formed a strong attachment to Miss Jane Bennet, the elder sister. The lady, while a fine young woman, unfortunately does not return his affection equally; given her family's connections and general deportment, this unequal attachment is of grave concern. I believe him to be sufficiently enamoured of Miss Bennet that he will offer for her, and it is my intention to remove to London to-morrow that I may give him to understand what he is about. You may therefore address future correspondence to Grosvenor Square.

I still mean to be at Pemberley on the eleventh December to escort you back to Town; hopefully by then this will all have blown over. Please forgive my brevity, Dearest, but there are many details to attend to, if, as I hope, I am to depart early to-morrow morning. May God bless,
Your loving brother,
Fitzwilliam Darcy

*****

FINIS

Books by Stanley Michael Hurd:

Darcy's Tale, Volume I: Into Hertfordshire
Darcy's Tale, Volume II: Into Kent
Darcy's Tale, Volume III: The Way Home

Darcy's Tale Deluxe Edition (All three volumes in one edition)

Made in the USA
San Bernardino, CA
27 September 2015